ALSO BY LIAN HEARN

TALES OF THE OTORI

Across the Nightingale Floor

Grass for His Pillow

Brilliance of the Moon

The Harsh Cry of the Heron

Heaven's Net Is Wide

Blossoms and Shadows

The Storyteller and His Three Daughters

THE TALE OF SHIKANOKO

Emperor of the Eight Islands

Autumn Princess, Dragon Child

Lord of the Darkwood

THE TENGU'S
GAME OF GO

THE TALE OF SHIKANOKO · BOOK 4

THE TENGU'S GAME OF GO

LIAN HEARN

FARRAR, STRAUS AND GIROUX   NEW YORK

Farrar, Straus and Giroux
18 West 18th Street, New York 10011

Printed in the United States of America
Originally published in 2016 by Hachette Australia
Published in the United States by Farrar, Straus and Giroux
First American edition, 2016

Map by K1229 Design

Library of Congress Cataloging-in-Publication Data
Names: Hearn, Lian, author.
Title: The Tengu's game of go / Lian Hearn.
Description: First American edition. | New York : Farrar, Straus and
    Giroux, 2016. | Series: The tale of Shikanoko ; book 4
Identifiers: LCCN 2016016693| ISBN 9780374536343 (paperback) |
    ISBN 9780374715045 (ebook)
Subjects: LCSH: Japan—History—1185–1600—Fiction. | BISAC:
    FICTION / Literary. | FICTION / Fantasy / General. | GSAFD:
    Fantasy fiction. | Adventure fiction. | Historical fiction.
Classification: LCC PR9619.3.H3725 T46 2016 | DDC 823/.914—dc23
LC record available at https://lccn.loc.gov/2016016693

Our books may be purchased in bulk for promotional, educational,
or business use. Please contact your local bookseller or the Macmillan
Corporate and Premium Sales Department at 1-800-221-7945, extension
5442, or by e-mail at MacmillanSpecialMarkets@macmillan.com.

www.fsgbooks.com • www.fsgoriginals.com
www.twitter.com/fsgbooks • www.facebook.com/fsgbooks

10   9   8   7   6   5   4   3   2   1

Let us all go forth
Bridle to bridle and see
No doubt the blossoms
Are scattering like snowflakes
In the ancient capital

—from *Kokin Wakashū: The First
Imperial Anthology of Japanese
Poetry*, translated by Helen Craig
McCullough

THE TALE OF SHIKANOKO
LIST OF CHARACTERS

MAIN CHARACTERS

Kumayama no Kazumaru, later known as Shikanoko
   or **Shika**

Nishimi no Akihime, the Autumn Princess, **Aki**

Kuromori no **Kiyoyori**, the Kuromori lord

Lady **Tama**, his wife, the Matsutani lady

Masachika, Kiyoyori's younger brother

Hina, sometimes known as Yayoi, his daughter

Tsumaru, his son

Bara or Ibara, Hina's servant

Yoshimori, also Yoshimaru, the Hidden Emperor, **Yoshi**

Takeyoshi, also Takemaru, son of Shikanoko and
   Akihime, **Take**

Lady **Tora**

Shisoku, the mountain sorcerer

Sesshin, an old wise man

The **Prince Abbot**
Akuzenji, King of the Mountain, a bandit
Hisoku, Lady Tama's retainer

THE MIBOSHI CLAN
Lord **Aritomo**, head of the clan, also known as the
    Minatogura lord
Yukikuni no **Takaakira**
The **Yukikuni lady**, his wife
Takauji, their son
Arinori, lord of the Aomizu area, a sea captain
Yamada Keisaku, Masachika's adoptive father
Gensaku, one of Takaakira's retinue
Yasuie, one of Masachika's men
Yasunobu, his brother

THE KAKIZUKI CLAN
Lord **Keita**, head of the clan
Hosokawa no **Masafusa**, a kinsman of Kiyoyori
Tsuneto, one of Kiyoyori's warriors
Sadaike, one of Kiyoyori's warriors
Tachiyama no **Enryo**, one of Kiyoyori's warriors
Hatsu, his wife
Kongyo, Kiyoyori's senior retainer
Haru, his wife
Chikamaru, later Motochika, **Chika**, his son
Kaze, his daughter

Hironaga, a retainer at Kuromori

Tsunesada, a retainer at Kuromori

Taro, a servant in Kiyoyori's household in Miyako

THE IMPERIAL COURT

The **Emperor**

Prince Momozono, the Crown Prince

Lady Shinmei'in, his wife, Yoshimori's mother

Daigen, his younger brother, later Emperor

Lady Natsue, Daigen's mother, sister of the Prince Abbot

Yoriie, an attendant

Nishimi no **Hidetake**, Aki's father, foster father to
    Yoshimori

Kai, his adopted daughter

AT THE TEMPLE OF RYUSONJI

Gessho, a warrior monk

Eisei, a young monk, later one of the **Burnt Twins**

AT KUMAYAMA

Shigetomo, Shikanoko's father

Sademasa, his brother, Shikanoko's uncle, now lord of
    the estate

Nobuto, one of his warriors

Tsunemasa, one of his warriors

Naganori, one of his warriors

Nagatomo, Naganori's son, Shika's childhood friend, later one of the **Burnt Twins**

AT NISHIMI
Lady Sadako and **Lady Masako**, Hina's teachers
Saburo, a groom

THE RIVERBANK PEOPLE
Lady Fuji, the mistress of the pleasure boats
Asagao, a musician and entertainer
Yuri, **Sen**, **Sada**, and **Teru**, young girls at the convent
Sarumaru, **Saru**, an acrobat and monkey trainer
Kinmaru and **Monmaru**, acrobats and monkey trainers

THE SPIDER TRIBE
Kiku, later Master Kikuta, Lady Tora's oldest son
Mu, her second son
Kuro, her third son
Ima, her fourth son
Ku, her fifth son
Tsunetomo, a warrior, Kiku's retainer
Shida, Mu's wife, a fox woman
Kinpoge, their daughter

Unagi, a merchant in Kitakami

SUPERNATURAL BEINGS
Tadashii, a tengu
Hidari and **Migi**, guardian spirits of Matsutani
The dragon child
Ban, a flying horse
Gen, a fake wolf
Kon and **Zen**, werehawks

HORSES
Nyorin, Akuzenji's white stallion, later Shikanoko's
Risu, a bad-tempered brown mare
Tan, their foal

WEAPONS
Jato, Snake Sword
Jinan, Second Son
Amcyumi, Rain Bow
Kodama, Echo

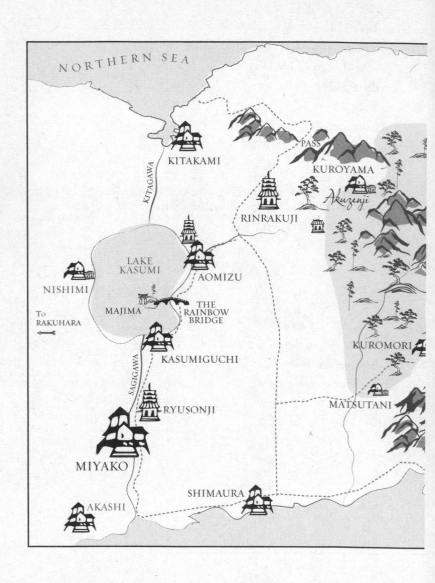

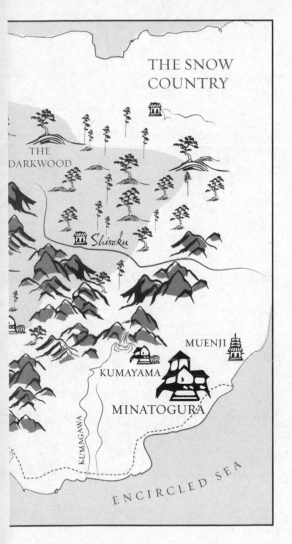

THE SNOW
COUNTRY

THE
DARKWOOD

Shisoku

----- ROADS

—— RIVERS
AND STREAMS

 CONVENT
OR TEMPLE

 HUT

SHRINE

ESTATE

 TOWN

MUENJI

KUMAYAMA

MINATOGURA

KUMAGAWA

ENCIRCLED SEA

THE TENGU'S
GAME OF GO

ARITOMO

"Yoshimori has been found?" For years Lord Aritomo had both dreaded and longed for this news. Until he saw Yoshimori's corpse with his own eyes he would never feel secure about Emperor Daigen's reign. Once Yoshimori was dead, preferably executed in public as the son of a rebel and traitor, no one would be able to question the legitimacy of Daigen. Even Heaven would have to concede.

He noticed Masachika recoil very slightly as he leaned toward him. Aritomo knew his breath smelled of decay and that his men feared he was grievously sick, even dying. He saw it in their sideways glances, their nervous voices. Yet not one of them had the courage to confront him with their fears. They did not understand he would outlive them all, that this passing illness was the price he was paying for immortality. He used white powder to mask his yellowing skin and madder to give color to his cheeks and lips. He drank wine to dull the pain and took many other potions, concocted for him by his physicians. Nothing could alleviate the night sweats and the vomiting, or restore healthy flesh to his gaunt frame, but it would all be worth it in the end.

"It may be just another rumor," Masachika replied. "Arinori reported it. Messengers came from Aomizu this morning. One of the owners of the pleasure boats, Lady Fuji, hinted that she knew where Yoshimori was."

"Is it worth investigating? It could be a ploy to ingratiate herself with Arinori. They will do anything to avoid paying their dues, these women."

"Indeed. And as we know the Aomizu lord is susceptible to such women, and inclined to be fanciful himself."

Aritomo raised his eyebrows. He did not encourage his men in criticism and backbiting. It corroded their loyalty to one another and eventually to him. But he was always interested in their opinions. He wondered what Arinori would have to say about Masachika in return. He would probably not be so quick to criticize, for Masachika had a reputation for acting swiftly against any perceived rival, wiping out offenses in blood.

Masachika said, "However, the woman died, probably poisoned. The most likely suspect, one of her entertainers, disappeared the next day, fleeing into the Darkwood. What if Fuji really did know something and was silenced?"

Aritomo shifted his jaw from side to side as he did when he was thinking. The dull clicking was the only sound in the room.

"You had better go to take a look," he said finally. "Wear unmarked clothes and don't draw attention to yourself."

He noticed with some satisfaction that Masachika was

galled by this. Masachika had acted as a spy for both the Miboshi and the Kakizuki, but Aritomo knew he would have preferred to leave all that in the past and play the part of a great lord and that he liked riding at the head of his retinue, with the pine trees of Kuromori and Matsutani emblazoned on surcoats, robes, and banners. Aritomo made a point of giving him minor errands, as though he were some insignificant underling, to keep him in his place. He saw Masachika hesitate as if he would refuse and continued to stare at him until the younger man submitted, bowed deeply, and took his leave.

He thinks he will bide his time and outlive me. But he will not. None of them will.

Yet he had to admit that he did not feel well. Often he passed sleepless nights, during which he recalled his years as an exile and fugitive, the murders of his young sons as hostages, the breakdown in health of his wife, leading to her early death. He knew he was seen as cold and unfeeling, but he had made himself so out of necessity, vowing he would never allow either love or grief to weaken him again. The last person he had cared for was Takaakira, who had hurt him so cruelly and made him weep for what he swore would be the last time.

Now hundreds served him in the capital and thousands more in the provinces and not one of them meant anything to him other than the means by which to impose his will. His scribes kept meticulous records of men, horses, weapons, and ships as well as all the various means of acquiring, maintaining, and transporting them. The administrative departments he had established kept the city running smoothly, supervised the different markets and guilds, burned refuse, carried out investigations, imposed imprisonment and other punishments. But all the time the Kakizuki loitered in Rakuhara, preventing him from bringing the entire realm under his control. Hearing of Yoshimori's existence would only embolden them.

Surely I am strong enough to annihilate them, he thought. *It is time to put my plan into action before these rumors reach them.* For some months he had been preparing ships and men, with the assistance of Arinori. Masachika's attempt to undermine his rival had had the opposite effect, confirming Aritomo's high regard for the seaman's qualities. He dictated a message to one of his scribes, telling Arinori to make the final preparations. If he sent it by boat it would reach Aomizu well before Masachika did.

He was still pondering the details of the attack when later that day he went to Ryusonji, as he often did since the Emperor and his mother had moved there. The halls and courtyards of the temple had been rebuilt, as well as the prison cells, and two spacious residences added, one for the Emperor and one for Lady Natsue. Daigen could have moved into the Imperial Palace, which had finally been finished, but the time never seemed right, and a string of excuses was made until it became obvious to Aritomo that Lady Natsue wanted to keep her son close by and under her control. She entertained Daigen and his court with many artistic pursuits, poetry contests, games of incense guessing and shell matching, and kept them amused with intrigues and gossip. Yet Aritomo knew that there was another side to her life, and it was this that interested him.

He also made time to visit Sesshin, who still sat in the cloister, played his lute, and sang to the dragon child. The old man rambled when he spoke at all and did not seem to know who Aritomo was, yet occasionally his gaze from under his sedge hat turned lucid, and then he let fall some fragment of ancient wisdom. Aritomo thirsted after these, collected them in his heart and brooded on them.

Once Sesshin had spoken of the dragon essence in the water of the well, Aritomo, remembering what Lady Natsue had said, drank it each day, even though his physicians feared it might have traces of poison in it. Another time Sesshin had seized him by his clothes, pulled him forward, and, speaking directly into his face, told him a recipe for lacquer tea, which Aritomo had made up, and swallowed as much as he could stomach every night. He interpreted Sesshin's utterances like prophecies, seeing in him a man who had no fear of death, since he knew he would live forever. He could not be bullied or coerced but was free in a way no one else was.

I will be like that, but I will not waste my immortality plucking a lute and singing songs. I will use it to impose my will on an entire realm.

It was a very hot afternoon. The Empress and her ladies sat in a pavilion by the stream. From a distance they made a pleasing picture in their light robes of summer colors of blue-green and mauve, brightly dressed attendants standing around with sunshades, but the stream had dried to a trickle and the moss was reduced to dust. When he looked more closely the women seemed enervated and under the white powder their faces gleamed with sweat.

Aritomo waited in the shade of the cloisters listening to the deafening drone of the cicadas. The Empress caught sight of him and made a sign to her ladies. They rose like a flock of dispirited plovers and prepared to move within. After a few moments one of them appeared at his side and asked him to follow her.

Inside the temple it was even hotter. He felt suddenly dizzy. The mingled scents of incense and lamp oil threatened to bring on nausea. The Empress was not in the reception room where he was usually taken but farther inside, in the very heart of the temple, a place devoted not to pleasure but to meditation and worship.

A few lamps burned on an altar, adding to the stifling heat of the room. Among the statues and images of deities he could make out a depiction of the Prince Abbot, the features shifting as the flames sent flickering shadows over the priest's face. So she worshipped him here, his sister, the Empress? She was still a beautiful woman but was becoming more like her brother as age melted the flesh from her bones, hollowed her cheeks, and domed her forehead.

She sat with her back to the altar, a carved armrest at her side. She barely acknowledged Aritomo's greeting before she spoke hurriedly.

"I am glad you came. I was about to send for you. I have something to show you."

She ordered the attendants to leave the room and then said in a low voice, "There is a text on the altar. Bring it to me."

He had knelt before her. Now he rose and, bowing again as he passed in front of her, did as she commanded. The text seemed very old, the pages dark indigo, the lettering gold. Dropping to his knees, he held it out to her.

She did not touch it but said, "Can you read it?"

He looked at the page he had opened. In the dark room it was like peering into the sky to read the stars. The characters were in an ancient style that he had trouble deciphering.

A voice spoke out of the darkness, from the ceiling, startling him, for he had thought they were alone—but surely it was no human voice that croaked harshly, "Yoshimori!"

Then the characters resolved themselves and he could read the name.

Yoshimori.

"It is the Book of the Future," Lady Natsue said. "With great difficulty, my brother inscribed my son's name there. Now Yoshimori's name has appeared and Daigen's has been erased."

Aritomo stared at the text in his hands. "Who has done this? Who has been allowed in here?"

"There is no need to come physically into this room to control the Book of the Future," she replied. "Or to write with the hands. It is with the power of the mind that the book is rewritten."

"Can it be changed? Can your son's name be reinstated?"

"Believe me, Lord Aritomo, I have been trying. But I have not succeeded yet."

Aritomo pondered this for a few moments and then said, "Some creature spoke just now. I heard Yoshimori's name."

"It was a werehawk. Two hatched out ten days ago. The eggs must have been lying beneath the altar for years. One day one of my priests noticed they were giving out heat. Soon after, cracks appeared in the shells. The birds came out fully fledged and within days were able to talk. They are insolent and aggressive, and too cunning to catch and kill. It is hard to bend werehawks to your will. My brother could do it, but I don't suppose anyone else is able to now."

There was a fluttering of wings and he felt the air move against his face.

"How do you train them?" He longed to have them at his command.

"I do not know. There is nothing written down. My priests have been searching, but so many records were lost in the fire."

"Maybe the old man knows," Aritomo said. "I will ask him."

"He must be made to leave." Natsue's voice was an angry hiss. "He may pretend to be witless, but every day I feel his powers increase and clash against mine. As fast as I learn, he learns faster. I am sure it is he who has rewritten the Book of the Future. You must get rid of him."

"It is hard to get rid of a man who cannot die."

"Then cut off his hands so he cannot write! Gag his

mouth, tear out his tongue so he cannot speak. Tie him up and throw him in a well!"

"I will have him confined somewhere else," Aritomo promised, thinking it would be to his own advantage to have Sesshin close by.

"Why have the werehawks hatched now?" Lady Natsue whispered. "Why has Yoshimori's name replaced Daigen's? What has changed? Can it be that Yoshimori has appeared? That he is alive?"

Above their heads the birds cackled as if they were laughing.

"There have been rumors," he said. "Masachika has gone to investigate. Yoshimori will be found, captured, and executed."

"Masachika, Kiyoyori's brother?"

"He delivered the Autumn Princess to us. If anyone can bring us Yoshimori, it will be him."

"Yet you neither trust nor like him," she said. "You have made that clear many times in our conversations."

"He has served me faithfully for many years. If he finds Yoshimori he will win my everlasting affection."

She was silent for a few moments. He wondered what was passing through her mind.

"You have no children, Lord Aritomo?"

The change of subject surprised him. "I had two sons, but they both died many years ago."

"You must know there are concerns about your health. What will happen to the realm after . . ."

"I can assure Your Majesty, I have no intention of dying!"

He could see his bluntness angered her, but all she said was "I look forward to hearing the news of Yoshimori's capture. I trust you will inform me immediately."

He promised he would. As he left, the werehawks swooped clumsily from the rafters and flew after him. On his way back through the many halls and courtyards he had been half-listening for the sound of the lute, and now he heard it, coming from the cloister that overlooked the lake.

Sesshin sat plucking the strings idly. He did not seem to play consciously and yet a tune emerged. The werehawks landed in front of him and opened their beaks, singing as if in harmony.

"Good day, my friends," Sesshin said, his fingers still. "What have you come to tell me?"

He turned his head toward Aritomo, and even though Aritomo knew the old man could not see him, his sightless attention unnerved him.

The birds warbled. Sesshin cocked his head, listening.

"The leaves are turning red," he said. "Yes, autumn is coming and all will be red."

Red was the color of the Kakizuki. It seemed hotter than ever in the cloister as the sun sank in the west. Aritomo's mouth was parched. He swallowed hard and said, "I could have you confined and tortured. It is by my grace that you are free."

"You could, you could," the old man agreed amiably. "But it will make no difference. The leaves will still turn red."

2

MASACHIKA

Masachika's spirits rose as he rode toward Aomizu. It was true Aritomo had been more than usually scornful to him and he had been made aware yet again that the lord to whom he had devoted his life disliked him intensely. Moreover, his head ached from the wine he had drunk the night before and his eyes, which had always been weak since the bees attacked him at Matsutani, were playing their usual tricks on him, one moment darkening as if he were going blind, the next perceiving people and animals, surrounded by flashing lights, that were not really there. Yet he felt the stirrings of confidence and hope. Maybe it was only a rumor, that Yoshimori had been found, but it could just as likely be true. If he were the one to deliver Yoshimori to Aritomo, as he had delivered the Autumn Princess, his standing would be assured and his rewards great. His secret desire, which he had never shared with anyone, not even his wife, Tama, was that Aritomo would make him his heir. Surely that would be a reasonable price to pay for the missing emperor?

But then I must also have heirs, he thought. Tama had fallen pregnant twice, but had not been able to carry either child to term, and now she was almost past childbearing. He still loved her and depended on her, but his lack of sons troubled him. Without them what was the point of being lord of three flourishing estates, let alone becoming Aritomo's successor? At times he regretted not having taken his former betrothed as a second wife; he feared Tama's jealousy and rage, but the idea of marrying another woman still persisted.

His reflections wandered to Kiyoyori's children, though he had not thought about them in years. Perhaps it was riding alongside Lake Kasumi that brought Hina to his mind, for she had drowned in its waters. It had been reported to him that a funeral was held, and his messenger had been shown the grave in Aomizu. And Kiyoyori's son had died at Ryusonji, though some strange legend had arisen about him and the dragon child. There were similar legends about Kiyoyori, whose body had never been found. Was it possible he had not died but was waiting to return and take his revenge? He often remembered reluctantly his dream of the foal. He had sent the young horse to Ryusonji with the others. After the Prince Abbot's death, Shikanoko had taken all three into the Darkwood. Was Kiyoyori still there, still Lord of the Darkwood? Would he come back with Shikanoko?

He shook himself and urged his horse on, riding fast as though he could escape these memories of the dead.

It was a week since the funeral, but the pleasure boats were still tied up at Aomizu. It seemed no one had taken charge since Lady Fuji's death. Masachika inspected the boats and then retired to a nearby temple, where he used Lord Aritomo's authority to commandeer a room and prepared to question the entertainers. It amused him that even though Aritomo had told him not to draw attention to himself, everyone was aware of his identity. He heard his name repeated through the courtyards and knew faces would pale, bowels loosen, and limbs tremble.

Most of them claimed they knew nothing, and he concluded they were telling the truth. They were divided in opinion over Lady Yayoi's guilt, some swearing that she had loved, even revered, Lady Fuji and was not capable of carrying out such an act of revenge, others claiming she had always been strange, different, too clever in some way, and had secretly resented her mistress. They had quarreled over a request. Moreover, she had many unusual skills, often treated people for all kinds of diseases, and was familiar with a wide range of herbs, both healing and dangerous.

Arinori attended most of the meetings. From the way he spoke of them, Masachika suspected he had some fondness for both women, probably had been intimately involved with them. There was nothing wrong with that, unless questions of regulations and tax had been overlooked, but he would keep it in mind. Arinori might not be quite so close to Lord Aritomo as he pretended, but Masachika liked to know as much about his rivals, and their weaknesses, as possible. He could already see several ways in which he could further undermine the Aomizu lord.

One young woman, Asagao, seemed to have known Yayoi best, and he questioned her at length.

"She said she was just going to the crossroads," Asagao said, tears trickling down her cheeks. She had wept almost continuously; her eyes were red, her lips swollen. Masachika felt the stirrings of attraction for her.

"But I knew she was lying." Asagao wiped her face with her sleeve. "When she said goodbye, I knew it would be forever."

"You had known her for a long time?"

"We were at the temple together when we were children. She must have been about twelve."

"And how many years ago was that?"

Asagao flushed a little and said, "I am now twenty-five, so twelve years ago."

"So long?" Masachika said, letting his eyes linger on her face, making her color deepen more. Then he addressed Arinori. "What do we know about this temple?"

"Lady Fuji kept young girls there until they were old enough to serve on the boats. I first went to it about twelve years ago, as it happens. It's probably just a coincidence, but the Abbess is the mother of the sorcerer they call Shikanoko."

"Oh yes, I remember now," Masachika said. "You went there to investigate. Was Yayoi there then?"

"She was," Arinori said. "As a matter of fact, she caught my eye. She was an exceptionally beautiful girl. I asked Lady Fuji to arrange that I might be her first . . ."

"And in return?" Masachika demanded.

"I have looked after them both, I admit, but there's been no conflict with my loyalty to our lord."

"I am sure," Masachika said smoothly. "I am not questioning your loyalty."

"As soon as Fuji hinted to me that she might know where Yoshimori was, I sent messengers to Miyako. I would have questioned her further myself, but unfortunately . . ." Again he let his sentence trail away, as though there were things he did not like talking about, words he feared uttering. Masachika noted this reluctance but said nothing, simply waited for Arinori to resume his account.

"When Yayoi did not return I assumed she had gone with the acrobats. I followed immediately, but there was no sign of them on the road. They had vanished. So I went on to the temple. I thought there might have been some kind of collusion between them. I knew Yayoi had been a great favorite of the Abbess."

"And?"

"I was angry. I'd always suspected that pack of women of subversion in some way. They offended me again and I learned nothing. I had the temple set on fire and the nuns fled. The Abbess was injured, but they took her with them."

Masachika turned his attention back to the young woman, who was crying even more. "Did either Fuji or Yayoi mention Yoshimori to you?"

"Who is Yoshimori?"

"The deceased emperor's grandson."

"No," Asagao said. "Why would they or anyone else here talk about any of the emperor's sons or grandsons? We are riverbank people. That world is as distant from us as the clouds are from the earth."

"Who was Yayoi?" Masachika questioned. "Where did she come from?"

"I can't tell you for sure. Most of us never talk about the past. But people used to say she was found in the lake—the acrobats pulled her and a baby boy from the water. The boy was brought up by them and still lives with them."

Pulled from the lake. Twelve years ago. Masachika said nothing for a few moments. His heartbeat had picked up. Was it possible? Had she not drowned after all? *I must have known. That is why I thought about her earlier.* Sometimes even he was amazed at the accuracy of his intuitions. And the boy—could he be the son of Akihime, the Autumn Princess? He remembered telling the Princess her son had drowned with Hina—how she had wept! But he had never told Aritomo about the child.

His voice when he spoke was made stern and cruel by these memories. "Where are these acrobats now? Why have they not been brought in for questioning?" He addressed Arinori, but it was Asagao who answered.

"They always go to the Darkwood at this time of year, to capture young monkeys."

"Do you think Yayoi went with them?"

"I suppose so," Asagao replied. "I don't know where else she would go—but I can't imagine her living as they do in the forest. She is like me, delicate, refined." She gave Masachika a look that was part challenging, part submissive, which he found quite charming. She was a truly beautiful young woman. He returned her look openly.

"Did she leave anything behind?"

"Almost everything. That's why no one thought she was

going to vanish. She even left her lute—she gave it to me and said I could play it. I brought it with me."

"Show me," Masachika said, but the shabby old instrument did not really interest him. Asagao, however, interested him very much. He liked the way sorrow and fear had bruised her. It made him want to grip her, leave his own imprint on her flesh. His wife's face floated for a moment before his eyes. He was away from home for long periods and had often taken advantage of the many women offered to him. They satisfied his physical needs, though none had ever touched him deeply. But this girl was different. He had always liked the riverbank women, and she seemed both exotic and vulnerable. She would be his reward for the inconvenience of the journey, for Aritomo's coldness and scorn. And the idea that she would give him a son fueled his desire.

"The Darkwood is part of my estate," he said. "As it happens, I plan to return to Matsutani to arrange a great hunt for Lord Aritomo, in the autumn. But men cannot spend all day and all night hunting—we need entertainment, too. I will take you and your lute with me. And Lord Arinori will pursue these acrobats and make sure Yayoi is not with them. Then we will arrange for the acrobats to be brought to Matsutani, as well. Lord Aritomo might find them amusing."

Arinori chuckled, and after Asagao had left to collect her belongings he said, "You have a taste for riverbank women, I see. I've had many a discussion as to which is the most beautiful, Yayoi or Asagao. I always had a slight preference for Yayoi."

Masachika cut him off, not wanting to consider they were on the same level. "Just how much did Fuji tell you?"

"Only what I said. She was going to propose a business deal; that's the sort of woman she was. She would not reveal anything more until she had settled the terms of the contract."

"All we can conclude, then, is that Yoshimori might be somewhere in the neighborhood?"

"Or anywhere around the lake. The boats travel great distances."

"No one has seen him for twelve years or more," Masachika said. "How would we even recognize him?"

"We could arrest and question every young man of the right age," Arinori suggested.

Masachika dismissed this with a wave of his hand. "Better to try to find Yayoi and question her."

"Well, I would undertake that, but I have other commitments. I am sure our lord has told you of the planned attack. I can't say too much. It's all highly secret."

Masachika struggled to hide the fact that he had no idea what Arinori was talking about.

"You may have noticed how few ships I have on the lake," Arinori said in a low voice. "They have all been sent to Akashi. And we have been building war vessels there for many months—but I must say no more. You never know who might be listening. There seem to be more spies and informants than ever. Everyone's always hoping to overhear something they can sell or use to their advantage."

"It is probably better that you are otherwise occupied,"

Masachika said, spitefully. "You have already done enough damage with your clumsy pursuit of Yayoi. We will send a message from Asagao, by means of those older men we already questioned, to bring the acrobats in the Darkwood to Matsutani, with the monkeys. Let's see if they can find Yayoi and report where she is without scaring her farther away. It's a shame your secret mission will prevent you from taking part in the hunt. It will be unlike any ever held in the history of the Eight Islands."

3

TAKEYOSHI

At first, Take's spirits were lowered by the death of the old woman, the grandmother he had never known. For a day or more he grieved, but then, the farther they walked, the more excited and elated he began to feel. He had always thought of himself as an orphan, a foundling of unknown parents. Now the idea that he might have a living father, and that his mother, though dead, had been a princess, thrilled him. Suddenly he seemed to understand everything about himself; his character and instincts all made sense. He felt the heft of the pole, the responding muscles in his arms and shoulders.

I am a warrior, born to fight. But now I need a teacher more than ever.

He felt he had grown taller. His gaze, as it continually swept the tangled trees for signs of danger, was more acute, his stride longer and more tireless, even his understanding was more perceptive. He was just thinking that the Emperor could be anywhere, and that the woman he knew as Lady Yayoi, or Older Sister, was the only person who knew, when Kon called from a high tree a little way ahead.

Take turned to watch the young men following. Noboru the monkey had switched to Yoshi's shoulder, and was affectionately grooming his hair. Saru was talking loudly and rapidly. Take could not hear what he was saying but could guess what it was, some involved anecdote, a ribald dream, a tale of seduction. Both young men laughed loudly, the sound ringing through the forest.

They should not laugh so loud! Take thought, as though trying to blind himself to the knowledge that had already pierced him like a ray of light. But it was blazing inside him and could not be ignored.

Yoshi!

I have a warrior's insight now, he thought. *How should I not know my lord, my prince, the ruler of this earthly realm I walk on?* And then he felt shocked and almost offended. It was an outrage that the son of Heaven, the heir to the Lotus Throne, should be ambling along a rough and dusty track, swapping dirty jokes, a monkey on his shoulder.

I will see him restored or die, he vowed solemnly. He could hardly prevent himself from running back and hurling himself at Yoshi's feet, swearing allegiance, offering him his life. It seemed the green light of the forest took on a new translucence, the birdsong became ravishingly beautiful. He gazed on Kon, finally understanding the bird's persistence. He heard nobility in the call now, and admired Kon's perseverance. The young Emperor had been lost, abandoned by everyone. Only Kon had stuck by him.

Kon and now me. I will take him as my example and be as true.

He found it hard to treat Yoshi naturally, and over the following days grew shy and deferential in his presence. Saru noticed it and teased him.

"Take has a crush on you," he whispered to Yoshi, loud enough for Take to hear. "I bet he has some juicy dreams! Why don't you share them, brat?"

It was obvious Saru had no idea—he could never have teased and insulted Yoshi if he had known who he was. It made Take decide that Yoshi could not know his true identity. If he had the slightest inkling he would not allow such familiarity. Saru's behavior upset and offended Take, but he said nothing, unsure what to reveal or when.

Yoshi became silent and withdrawn, as though a great weight had settled on his shoulders.

A feeling of coldness, almost enmity, began to grow between Take and Saru. All his life Take had admired the young acrobat, as if Saru were his older brother. Now he became aware of the immense gulf between them. He could not help seeing himself differently: his father was a warrior, his mother a princess. Saru was a nobody from the insignificant village of Iida. Yet these thoughts troubled him and he was half-ashamed of them, for in the world of the acrobats talent and ability were all that mattered, and in these Saru far outstripped him. He still admired him, but he found Saru crude and resented his friendship with Yoshi, seeing how demeaning it was.

They drew near the hot springs and began to notice signs of the monkeys' presence—broken twigs and half-eaten fruit on the ground, chattering in the treetops. Noboru became agitated and screeched most of the day. The young men set up camp. They swam in the hot pools, climbed trees, and every day practiced acrobatics, tumbling across the clearing, swinging from branches like monkeys. Take joined them, but his old carefree exuberance was gone.

I will never be an acrobat, he thought, looking at their slight, wiry frames. He was already as tall as Yoshi, taller than Saru. *I will never perform again.*

The lady—he did not really want to use her old name and she had not told him her true one—retreated from them, telling them she would spend the days reading, fasting, and meditating. He wanted to talk more to her, to question her about everything, but her reserve discouraged him. She came every morning to collect fresh water, but otherwise stayed out of sight. Occasionally Take heard her chanting but he did not know what the words meant. He had only ever heard her sing ballads of love before. He took to sleeping nearby in case anything threatened her in the dark, but both day and night were peaceful. Nobody came.

Saru was enjoying his time in the forest and was in no hurry to make their capture and go home. But Yoshi's silence increased and Take knew the lady was waiting for something, someone, some sign. He himself was restless. He wanted to start his new life as a warrior. But who could teach him all he needed to know? He had never stopped thinking about Kinpoge and her father. *He turned me away once, but I was too easily discouraged. Maybe it was a test of some sort. Now I am back in the forest I should try again.*

The tension between him and the two young men became

almost unbearable. He was overpolite to Yoshi, overrude to Saru, irritating them both equally. There seemed to be no way to resolve the situation. The knowledge that the Emperor of the Eight Islands lived, ate, slept alongside him was too momentous to contain. He knew he was in danger of blurting out a secret that was not his to tell. One night, after Saru's teasing had turned particularly malicious, he made the decision that he would go back to the man who had been taught by the tengu and insist that he teach him—this time he would not be refused.

He set out very early the next morning, before anyone else was awake. He walked swiftly, imagining all the things he longed to have: red-laced armor, a helmet crowned with stag antlers or boar tusks, a long sword forged by a master, so sharp it would slice through silk, a bow with nineteen arrows in a quiver, a white stallion for a warhorse. He practiced declaiming his name as warriors did at the onset of battle.

I am Kumayama no Takeyoshi, son of Shikanoko, grandson of Hidetake . . .

His voice, just beginning to change to its adult timbre, echoed through the forest, but the chorus of cicadas was the only response. Now and then there was the sound of a large animal crashing through the bushes. *Wild boar,* he thought, hoping to kill one and take its tusks but also fearing its ferocious power. He knew the boar was the most dangerous animal in the forest.

At first, he followed the stream as he had done previously. It was not long before he came to a tree that he was fairly sure was the one where he had met Kinpoge. After that, a landslip of several boulders blocked his way. The stream, reduced to a trickle, came seeping out under them, but the gap was too small for Take to squeeze through and, furthermore, it looked like the sort of place where water spirits might dwell, and he did not want to be seized by one and kept captive for years and years. The rocks' surface was perfectly smooth, with no handholds or footholds. There was nothing he could do but leave the stream and try to walk around them. He walked until nightfall, slept restlessly, and then rose at dawn.

It was a dull, overcast day and in the dim greenish light it was impossible to be certain of the right direction. The forest had changed in a year. Trees had fallen, new ones had grown rapidly, vines had spread, undergrowth had thickened. Take would not admit to himself that he was lost; he kept walking, slashing at the undergrowth with his pole, listening for the sound of water. The air was thick with moisture and one bird kept piping monotonously. Excitement had kept him awake the previous night and now his eyes began to feel heavy, as if he had fallen asleep and was dreaming. Into his mind came a series of pictures; he thought he heard someone call his name, his feet stumbled. As he recovered his balance, he saw a woman standing a short distance ahead of him.

"Kinpoge?" he said uncertainly. It was so long since he had seen her that he could not be sure of recognizing her. At first he thought it was her, grown taller and older, and then, as he came closer, he knew it was not. He remembered

Kinpoge as bright and pretty, but this woman was the most beautiful he had ever seen, with pale skin, red lips, and hair so long and thick it covered her like a silky shawl. Her tiny white feet emerged from it like little flowers and he felt an almost uncontrollable urge to kneel before her and touch them with his lips.

"A young warrior!" the woman said, her voice as charming and melodious as a songbird's. "Come, let me take you to my house. I will give you food and wine."

Take refused politely, saying, "Thank you, I must not inconvenience you. But I am looking for a girl and her father. They live somewhere around here—do you know them? I'd be very grateful if you could direct me to their place."

The woman made a sound like a hiss and her tongue flickered in her perfectly formed mouth.

"Come with me and refresh yourself. Then I will set you on your way."

She held out her hand and Take, suddenly realizing he was unbearably hungry and thirsty, was about to take it, when there was a clattering overhead, a shower of leaves and twigs fell, and the skull horse, Ban, with Kinpoge clinging to it, landed on the ground in front of him.

"Don't let her touch you!" she shrieked, as she let go of Ban and pushed Take back. He lost his footing and dropped the pole, but turned his fall into a backward roll and came up on his feet, grabbing the pole and brandishing it. Kinpoge turned to face the woman and said a few words that Take did not understand. The woman's head flattened and her body stretched out, sucking her limbs and her tiny feet up into it. She hissed again, her snake tongue spitting at them, before her huge, brightly patterned shape slithered away between the vines.

"She will be very disappointed," Kinpoge said. "She probably hasn't run across a young man in years."

"What was she?" Take said.

"A snake woman—a sort of ghost. She has an insatiable appetite for sex, but she sucks her lovers dry and then casts them aside like snakeskins. Luckily for you Ban and I came along when we did."

"I wasn't taken in by her," Take said. "I would never have gone with her." But his heart was pounding with fear and regret.

"Fine! You can look after yourself. That's why you're wandering around lost. I suppose you were coming to find us? I'll meet you at home." She grabbed Ban's reins and clicked her tongue at him. As the skull horse rose into the air, Take cried, "Wait! I'm sorry. It's true, I am lost. That is, I'm not sure of the way. Please go with me."

The horse hovered. She called, "Say, 'Thank you, Kinpoge, for saving me from the snake woman.'"

He repeated the words and added, smiling, "I am very pleased to see you again."

"Really? Or is it just that you want my father to teach you?"

"I am pleased, really," he said.

Ban came slowly down and Kinpoge slid off. "So you don't want to learn from my father?"

"Of course I do! Can't both be true?"

"Once you start learning from my father, you won't care for me anymore," Kinpoge said, giving him a mournful look.

"He'll probably turn me away again," Take said, as they began to walk back the way he had come.

"No, he has been waiting for you," Kinpoge said.

"He has? What made him change his mind?"

"You'll have to ask him," she returned.

The hut was still a long day's walk away. Mostly he followed Kinpoge, but where the forest allowed they walked side by side.

"My real name is Takeyoshi," he said on one of these times.

"I know, and your father is the one they call Shikanoko."

"How did you know that?" he exclaimed. "I only found out a few days ago myself."

"The tengu told my father. Tengu seem to know most things."

"I hope I will meet the tengu," Take said.

"Be careful what you hope for," Kinpoge replied.

They crossed the stream and walked into the clearing. Take stood still for a few moments, looking around, taking in the carved animals, the rock shapes, covered in moss, that suggested bears or wild boars. Then he saw the dogs, both real and fake. They looked back at him, the real dogs yapping, the fake ones voiceless. He felt a strong revulsion for their moth-eaten coats, their awkwardly angled limbs, their gemstone eyes.

Two men sat by the fire. The sound of rasping echoed through the clearing. He saw they were sharpening tools: axes, knives, and—his heart bounded—swords. They worked in silence, swiftly and competently. They were very similar in build and appearance. Both had long, wispy beards and mustaches, and their thick hair fell to their shoulders. They used their feet, with thin, flexible toes, as much as their hands. They wore only loincloths and their skin, turned copper by the sun, glistened with sweat.

"Come on!" Kinpoge said, and then called out, "Father! Look who I found!"

One of the men got to his feet, laying aside the tools unhurriedly. He moved a few paces away from the fire and stood waiting for Take to approach him.

Take went forward warily. He gripped the pole, wondering if he should prostrate himself before the man he hoped would be his teacher, deciding it would do no harm, but before he could bend his knees, the pole flew from his hands, struck him on the head, and landed some distance away. The man he had been about to kneel to was now behind him. He spun around, but caught only a glimpse of him before he disappeared.

The man by the fire was grinning and Kinpoge was doubled over with laughter.

"You've no idea how funny you looked," she cried.

Her father reappeared beside her. "It could be quite amusing to have a pupil," he said.

Take felt rage building within him. He struggled not to let it overcome him. He remembered the old priest's words the day they had left Aomizu. *Master your anger*, he had said. Here, he would need more than ever the wisdom and the ability to discern what was real.

"If you do permit me to become your pupil, I will be forever grateful," he said, using formal speech, "and I will endeavor to continue to amuse you."

Kinpoge's father chuckled again. "You look like a strong lad, agile, too. I think you will learn quickly. And you will have to, for my friend Tadashii tells me we do not have much time. Of course, it's hard to tell, as time moves differently in the world of the tengu, but nevertheless . . . You've already met my daughter. I am Mu, this is my brother, Ima. We are your brothers, too, in a way, but I'll explain all that later. Who are you traveling with?"

"The lady who was called Yayoi, and the acrobats Sarumaru and Yoshimaru." He did not want to say anything that would give away Yoshi's true identity, but Mu said, as if he already knew, "Yoshimaru? Well, he should be as safe in the Darkwood as anywhere, for the time being. Kinpoge, go with Ban and find them. Tell them Takeyoshi is staying with me for a while. Reassure the lady that he is in no danger. And now, Takeyoshi, since we have no time to waste, let's get to work."

4

MASACHIKA

Masachika gazed on Lord Aritomo with an emotion close to pity, not one he often experienced. It was indeed cruel for the lord to be attacked by what appeared to be an incurable illness at this time when so much power lay in his hands. No one seemed to be able to diagnose or treat it. Aritomo himself spoke of it lightly, brushing aside his retainers' concerns, all the while smiling as if he had a precious secret that he would tell no one. Masachika knew his lord had special teas brewed—Aritomo was sipping one now—but he did not know what was in them and had never been invited to share them.

Aritomo had deteriorated in the weeks Masachika had been away in Aomizu, yet as usual he made no mention of his failing health nor, his aides whispered to Masachika, had he allowed it to interfere with his devotion to government. He rose while it was still dark and did not retire until late at night. The best way to win his gratitude, people joked, was to donate lamp oil or candles, or fireflies in cages. But no one made jokes in his presence.

Masachika had written a report for Lord Aritomo, which the lord was now perusing carefully, but it was not as detailed and comprehensive as it might have been nor had he lingered over its telling. He said there was no way to assess the rumor, but he was taking steps to have the fleeing suspect tracked down. He did not mention that she might be Kiyoyori's daughter. He would save that valuable piece of information for the right moment. He told himself he did not want to tire or place additional strain on his lord, but the truth was he was impatient to get back to the girl called Asagao, who had cast a spell over him. He had been afraid it would not last, that since she was just a woman of pleasure he would tire of her as quickly as he had been ensnared by her, but, during the hot summer nights when the skies were like velvet and the stars like pearls, she aroused in him an intoxicating ecstasy, an insatiable thirst. She made him feel like a young man again. From time to time he wondered with feelings of dread what would happen if Tama were to find out about her, and he recalled all his wife's fine qualities with regret, but his new passion had rendered him helpless. He would never give Asagao up.

He tried not to think of her now; he shifted uncomfortably in his formal kneeling position, summoned up images of snow, icy waterfalls . . .

Aritomo had put the report down and was scrutinizing him with his shrewd gaze. Masachika feared the lord might see right through him and, hoping to distract him, said,

"Lord Aritomo will be well enough to ride to Matsutani in the autumn? I am arranging a hunt in your honor. The air, the excitement, the hot springs will restore your health, I am sure. We will have deer, and wild boar, bears, possibly, and wolves. I will also provide hawks and falcons—anything you might desire."

He decided to keep the entertainment he had in mind, the musicians and the acrobats with their monkeys, to himself for the time being. He wanted it to be a complete surprise.

"I will come," Aritomo said. "I feel a longing for the forest and the open air. It will be an opportunity to reward those loyal to me and to assess my warriors' skills." He paused for a moment, then gestured to Masachika to come closer. He said quietly, "I am going to deal with the Kakizuki before winter comes. It will coincide nicely with your hunt. We will let their spies think we are fully occupied with sport and entertainment, but I have already dispatched a fleet of ships, carrying hundreds of men, to take them by surprise. Ari nori is in command."

He grinned at Masachika. His breath smelled of his illness. "They think the old badger is finished, but he is still craftier than them."

So that was Arinori's secret mission!

"It is a brilliant idea, but I should be leading such an attack force," Masachika said with feigned enthusiasm. "I can delegate the hunt to someone else."

"If you and I seem otherwise occupied, we will allay suspicions," Aritomo replied. "Besides, Arinori has skills as a sailor and an admiral. Once the Kakizuki are eliminated, these rumors about Yoshimori will disappear." He tapped the report with his forefinger. "Rumors arise all the time. Usually there is no substance to them. An emperor with no one to fight for him is hardly an emperor."

"Indeed," Masachika agreed.

"Don't be disappointed. You will have your chance in land fighting soon enough. When the Kakizuki are gone, we will take care of Takauji."

Masachika shuffled backward out of Aritomo's presence, touching his head to the floor once more as attendants slid open the doors behind him. Outside, in the wide corridor, he stood and adjusted his robe. Then, trying not to look as if he was hurrying, he began to walk back to where his grooms waited with the ox carriage.

However, as he left the outer courtyard, passing through the great gates with their carvings of lions, someone approached him. It was a man he knew vaguely, a minor official in the Emperor's household, though he could not recall his name. Masachika suspected he probably wanted to discuss something about money. The Emperor never seemed to have enough and was always asking for more. Then he remembered: *Yoriie*.

Masachika's bodyguards had also been waiting outside and now began to move closer to him, their hands on their swords. Surely they did not suspect old Yoriie of an assassination attempt? He made a sign to them to hold back and greeted the official as curtly as he could, without being downright rude.

Yoriie replied more fulsomely. "If it is not too great an inconvenience, would Lord Masachika accompany me to Ryusonji?"

His manner was obsequious, but his small eyes were sharp and seemed to flicker upward to scrutinize Masachika. The residences at Ryusonji were luxurious and expensive, yet ministers received a stream of complaints about the accommodation. It was too hot or too cold, the roof leaked, the nearby river stank, there was an invasion of biting fleas, owls hooted all night.

Masachika assumed it would be another of these and groaned inwardly, but he reminded himself that no one survived in an official position in the capital without brains, courage, or wealth, preferably all three, and that he should not underestimate Yoriie nor refuse the Emperor. Regretfully he again put aside his desire and agreed to go with Yoriie, inviting him to ride in the ox carriage.

They did not speak much as the ox made its slow, laborious way through the crowded streets toward the river. The Sagigawa had all but dried up and lay in a series of stagnant pools that, Masachika noted, keeping his mouth firmly closed, did indeed smell noxious. The townspeople threw refuse in the river, which normally would be washed away rapidly but which now lay decomposing, picked over by scavenging crows and wild dogs.

Outside Ryusonji's gates, people milled—beggars seeking alms, the sick and crippled praying for healing, amulet sellers, and pilgrims. Since it had become the Emperor's residence, the whole temple had taken on an increased aura of sacredness. Slivers of wood were carved from the gates, pebbles stolen from the paths, leaves gathered from the ginkgo and sakaki trees, all with the hope that they would provide talismans against ill health and misfortune. Partly for this reason, the buildings and gardens had a dilapidated and untended look.

Two large black birds perched on the roof and peered down at Masachika with golden eyes. One of them made a derisive cackle and the other echoed it. They sounded uncannily human. Their excrement had whitened the gate and the ground below.

The luxury of the inner rooms tried to compensate for the external decay, but nothing could remove the stench from the river. The great shutters were all closed, presumably to keep it out, and the dim interior was lit by oil lamps, the smoke making the rooms even hotter.

There was a large hall within his residence, where usually the Emperor received visitors, sitting on a raised dais behind a thin, gilded bamboo screen, his courtiers ranked on the steps beneath him, but this time Yoriie indicated Masachika should follow him to the other side of the temple, where he had never been before.

The official stepped up on the veranda of another beautiful residence and called softly. "Lord Masachika is here."

The door slid sideways, opened by unseen hands. Masachika dropped to his knees on the threshold and bowed his head to the ground.

There was a rich scent that he could not quite identify, and for a moment he thought with a surge of emotion that it must be the Emperor himself, kneeling on an embroidered silk cushion, not five paces from him. Then the figure removed the covering from its face and spoke. It was a woman.

"Lord Masachika, thank you for coming. I presume you know who I am?"

He could only guess, never having seen her before. "Our sovereign's noble mother," he said, raising his head briefly and then lowering it again. Natsue, the Emperor's mother, sister to the Prince Abbot. "In what way can I serve you, Your Majesty?"

"Can I trust you to keep this conversation secret? Will you swear to me that you will speak of it to no one?"

He hesitated, aware of Yoriie just behind him, of the courtiers, the servants in the background, any one of whom might be a spy. Was it some kind of trap, some test of his loyalty? "I can have no secrets from Lord Aritomo," he said guardedly.

"How is our dear lord and protector?" she said. "We have heard his recovery is slow."

"Alas, slower than we all desire, but he does not allow his illness to impede him in any way. No man has a stronger will."

"A strong will means nothing if Heaven is against you," Lady Natsue replied. "My son and I are deeply concerned for the welfare of the country and the people. Is it possible that Lord Aritomo's illness is a punishment of some sort?"

"I cannot speak for Heaven, Your Majesty. Let your priests do that."

"But they have, Lord Masachika. Oh yes, indeed they

have. We have heard rumors that Yoshimori might still be alive. People have the audacity to say he has greater legitimacy than my son."

"We are doing our best to stamp out such treason," Masachika murmured.

"Yet the drought continues, and with it the unrest. But Yoshimori's death, if it were confirmed or, better still, publicly witnessed, would make my son the rightful emperor. Why has Lord Aritomo not achieved this?"

When Masachika did not reply she went on, "I believe his illness is making him less than capable."

He dared to raise his eyes and stare at her. She held his gaze for a moment, smiling slightly. "I had thought . . . but you are a loyal man, Masachika. I will not trouble you further."

Now he was intrigued. He very much wanted to know what she had thought. "Lord Aritomo does not need extra burdens," he heard himself say. "I will keep whatever you want to confide in me to myself."

"My son and I admire you," Lady Natsue said. "We wonder if Lord Aritomo fully appreciates you. It is wrong that he should not trust you. The Emperor would like you to be closer to him. We are both worried about Lord Aritomo's health. That is the only reason, you understand . . ."

That you are choosing me to replace him? The idea was preposterous, yet he was sure it was what she was hinting at. The heavy scent, the stifling room were making Masachika light-headed.

"It is a shame Lord Aritomo has no sons," Lady Natsue

said. "Were he to pass away there would be grave danger that the realm would once more be torn apart by war. We must make the succession clear."

It was exactly what Masachika hoped for, but he did not trust himself to speak.

"My son is not happy with his circumstances. He is bored. He is intelligent, you know, and thinks deeply. He does not want to be someone else's figurehead. He wants to feel he is truly the ruler of this great country, like the warrior emperors of ancient Shin. He needs loyal men like yourself to serve him, in positions of influence and power." She spoke obliquely, leaving essential things unsaid. Masachika had to fill in the gaps himself—but was it truly her meaning or was he allowing his own desires to interpret her words?

"I am forever his servant as I am yours," he said. "But what will you have me do? I have only a few men at my command . . ." There was no way he could mount a full-scale rebellion and he was not such a fool, or so ambitious, that he would hint at such an act, even if only to deny it.

"Do nothing for the time being," Lady Natsue said. "Simply make sure Lord Aritomo's sickness is well managed."

Does not improve, he translated silently.

"And be ready for our instruction. That is all."

He bowed again to her and prepared to leave, but she made a sign to her attendants. Two women shuffled forward silently and helped her stand. One of them took the shawl, the other adjusted her many-layered robe, pink lapped over green, green over red, and so on through twelve or more different colored layers. She was a tiny woman, made all the more tiny by the mass of clothes. Her hair reached to the ground, adding even more weight to bow her down. She had grown thin, but her skin was still white, her lips red. He remembered that in her youth she had been a beautiful woman who had won the deceased emperor's heart.

"Follow me," she said. "My son wishes to let his eyes rest on you."

She moved smoothly and swiftly, as though not walking at all but carried by unseen beings. As she passed him, Masachika, still prostrate, smelled her perfume even more strongly. It seemed to suggest infinite possibilities.

He walked at a respectful distance behind her down the long corridor. It was open on one side, giving out onto a courtyard. In the center was a large fishpond fringed with reeds and lotus leaves. *I must discuss all this with Tama*, he thought, as he followed Lady Natsue into the private chambers of the Emperor.

After a short, enigmatic interview in which the Emperor spoke obliquely of poetry and the weather, Yoriie accompanied Masachika to the gate, where the birds again looked down at him and seemed to jeer. He even thought he heard one speak his name.

"What are those birds?" he asked. "Where did they come from?"

"The priests tell us they are werehawks," Yoriie replied. "The eggs hatched recently. The deceased Prince Abbot used to own several, and they flew far and wide at his bidding, but none remained after his death and now no one knows how to train them."

"What about Master Sesshin? He would know."

"He is in his dotage and useless," Yoriie said, his mouth curling in irritation. "He found their antics amusing and spoiled them, giving them food. I suppose he might have been able to command them, but he is no longer here."

"I thought I had not heard him playing. Where is he?"

"Her Majesty disliked him and wanted him removed. Lord Aritomo's men took him away."

Masachika frowned. His intuition told him there was something strange going on, that he should look into it further, but then he thought of Asagao, longed to be with her, and could not bear any further delay.

5

MU

Take was a quick learner. It was as if the knowledge lay hidden within him and all Mu had to do was bring it to the surface. Mu was as fierce and as strict as the tengu had been with him, but Take accepted his discipline without question. He seemed to soak up everything; no challenge was too great. If he could not master some technique with the sword, or some practice of meditation, he worked obsessively at it, until he understood what Mu was asking of him and could achieve it.

Mu admired his pupil and had become fond of him. Ima liked him, and the animals, fake and real, came to accept him. Take in return treated them all with respect and kindness.

"Everything's going fine," Mu told Tadashii on one of the tengu's visits. Take had not yet met him, as the tengu always came after the boy had fallen into one of the short sleeps of exhaustion Mu allowed him. "Except I am worried about my daughter. She likes him too much. What will I do if she falls in love with him? We share the same father—the relationship is too close. He is a young warrior and she is the daughter of a fox woman. I don't want her to be hurt."

"I told you, I am no expert in these matters," Tadashii said. "It's easy enough to separate them. I'll take Shikanoko's son away with me for a while. And, since you will be visiting your brother soon, you can take Kinpoge with you. If she wants a man, let her marry one of her cousins."

"I will be visiting my brother?" Mu repeated. "I can tell you, that's not going to happen."

"I believe it is," Tadashii replied. "Where is Shikanoko's son?"

"Asleep by the stream. You're not taking him now?"

"No time like the present," Tadashii said, unfurling his wings and flexing them. "He must be ready for us."

He flew as silently as an owl to the stream, picked up the sleeping boy with one hand, called out a farewell, and disappeared above the treetops.

Even Mu, who had come to know Tadashii well over the years, was startled by this abrupt departure. Kinpoge, when she woke the next morning, was inconsolable.

"Where did the tengu take him? Why? When will he come back?" She was fighting back tears.

"It's part of his training." Mu tried to reassure her. "He will be fine. You remember Tadashii often took me away. Didn't I always come back?"

"You are an adult. You can look after yourself. Take is only a boy," she argued.

"Take can look after himself very well," Ima told her. "He has grown up in the weeks he has been here." He tried to put Kinpoge on his knee to comfort her, but she struggled from his grasp.

"You sent him away to spite me!" she accused her father angrily. "You don't want us to be friends!"

"Maybe I don't, but so what? You are too young to know what is best for you. And anyway, girls should obey their fathers." Mu tried to maintain his composure. Only Kinpoge could unsettle him so much. He closed his eyes, breathed deeply, seeking to enter the state of no attachment that made him the warrior of nothingness. He heard Kinpoge sigh in exasperation and walk away. He heard the clink of Ban's bridle and the slight rush of air as the skull horse took off.

Tadashii is right. If she is to be married the only appropriate bridegroom will be one of her cousins.

A dog began to bark. Ima said, "Someone is coming."

Mu heard the sounds at the same time: twigs breaking, leaves rustling, the four-beat step of horses. He opened his eyes.

Chika rode into the clearing on a tall brown horse, leading another smaller gray, laden with baskets. He was wearing a green hunting robe with a chrysanthemum crest, a bow on his back, a sword at his hip. Despite his mustache and beard, Mu recognized him at once, though years had passed since the day he had last seen him when Tsunetomo, the one-eyed warrior, had slung his youngest brother, Ku, unconscious, over the back of his horse and had ridden away with Kiku, Kaze, and Chika, leaving Mu destroyed in body and heart.

Mu let the memory reform in his mind, looking at it dispassionately, observing how he had recovered from it and how it had given him the strength he now possessed. At the same time, he studied Chika, seeing the boy he had been, the man he had become. Kiku, he thought, had given him something he needed, some love or approval. He supposed they were now brothers-in-law. Yet there was still an emptiness within him, some unfulfilled longing that was on the point of hardening into bitterness. Nothing would ever satisfy him, no honors or rewards would ever heal the wound dealt to the heart of a child.

It was frustrating to know there was so much he could teach Chika, and to recognize at the same time that Chika was unteachable.

I am thinking like a tengu! The idea surprised and shocked him.

Ima had walked toward the visitor. Chika dismounted, greeted him briefly, and handed the horses' reins to him. Then he came close to Mu, standing somewhat defiantly in front of him.

Mu acknowledged him with a slight inclination of his head. "What are you doing here, Chika?"

His familiar tone seemed to annoy the other man. Mu could see he had become touchy and proud. Chika glanced around, surveying the clearing and the hut.

"Not much has changed, I see."

"Not much," Mu agreed. "And yet, everything."

"And you?" Chika turned his gaze back to Mu. "You seem to have suffered no lasting harm."

"I did and I did not."

"It was I who saved your life, you know. I think I deserve some gratitude. Tsunetomo wanted to kill you."

Mu bowed. "You were indeed the instrument of Heaven's will."

"So don't forget, you are indebted to me," Chika said.

"If there is a debt it will be paid," Mu replied. "But by the same currency, if there is an offense it will be avenged."

Chika stared at him blankly.

"What can I do for you?" Mu said.

"Let's sit down and talk," Chika said. "Perhaps Ima could make us some tea. I've brought leaves with me, if you have none. We import them from Shin. I also have presents for you and your daughter. The gray horse is yours. Ima, tether the horses and unpack the baskets. They are all gifts from Kiku, your brother."

"I know very well who Kiku is," Ima muttered under his breath as he set a pot of water to boil on the fire. The tea leaves were of the highest quality, fragrant and sharp-flavored. Among the gifts were green ceramic cups, much finer than anything Mu had ever drunk from.

"Your brother is deeply sorry for what happened," Chika said, after taking a sip. "He asks you to forgive him. He wants to see you."

"If he is so sorry, why did he not come himself?" Mu replied. The moment he spoke he regretted his pettiness. He was going to visit Kiku, he knew that: the tengu had said so.

There was no need to pretend he needed persuading. On the other hand, it would do no harm to seem reluctant.

"You don't know what Master Kikuta has become, or you wouldn't suggest that," Chika replied. "His empire is now so great he can't just leave it to travel to the Darkwood."

"Where is this empire?"

"In Kitakami, on the north sea."

"From whence he summons his subjects into his presence," Mu said, with a hint of sarcasm.

"He doesn't consider you his subject, Mu."

"Then what does he consider me?"

"His brother, whom he wronged."

"Those were his words?"

"Exactly as he spoke them," Chika said, with such sincerity Mu knew he was lying.

"I will come with you," he said finally. "We should meet again, Kiku and I, and Kuro and Ku as well. What about you, Ima? Will you come, too?"

"Someone has to look after the animals," Ima said, "and keep an eye on the hut. I have no desire to leave the Darkwood and go to Kitakami. Besides, Kiku did not send a horse for me."

Was he hurt by the oversight? It was impossible to tell. As always, Ima's calm expression gave no hint of his true feelings. Mu remembered what the tengu had said. *Don't feel sorry for him.* He was pierced by an emotion that was not pity, though pity was included in it. *I love him*, he realized. *Is this what brothers feel for each other?*

"We'll have to wait for Kinpoge to return," he said.

"She'll come back soon," Ima said, smiling. "She took off without eating; she'll be hungry."

As Ima predicted, Kinpoge appeared not long after. Chika produced presents for her: a robe of cream silk embroidered with celandines and aconites; sweet bean paste; a small bronze mirror into which she gazed in wonder; an exquisite carving of a horse, one foot raised, with a long mane and tail. Mu was astonished at the luxury and wealth that the gifts indicated and also at how well chosen they were, how apt for Kinpoge. He asked who had been responsible.

Chika addressed Kinpoge. "My sister, Kaze, chose them for you. Do you remember her? She knew you when you were a little girl. She always kept a fondness for you. She has many children herself—your cousins. You will meet them in Kitakami."

"Can they do the things Father and I can do?" Kinpoge asked.

Chika looked at Mu, eyebrows raised.

"She means invisibility, the second self, that sort of thing," Mu explained.

"Oh, they are all experts in that!" Chika laughed. "You never know who is who or where any of them are."

Kinpoge whispered to her father, "I do want to meet them, but what about Take? He'll come back, and we won't be here."

"Ima will tell him where we've gone. Anyway, we don't know how long he will be away with the tengu. We're not going forever, just for a visit. It will make time go faster until you see Take." He knew he was not being completely truthful with her. The reality was that he hoped she would never meet Take again.

"Can I take Ban?" she asked.

"Ban is going to stay with me," Ima said. "You are going to ride a real horse, that pretty gray."

Kinpoge looked at the horse, with shining eyes. It seemed to notice her gaze, raised its head, and whickered to her. She went to it and patted its neck.

"Let's get going," Chika said. "It's not yet noon. We've several hours of daylight left."

Kinpoge ran to Ban and gave the skull horse a pat. It quivered all over and its eye sockets seemed to widen. Then she hugged her uncle. Mu embraced Ima, too.

"Take care of yourself," he said.

As they rode away, he saw an old vixen on the edge of the forest. He did not know if she was Kinpoge's mother, Shida. Was it possible that she was still alive? All that day he was aware that she followed them, but the next morning she was gone.

A week later they were in Kitakami. Autumn came early to the northern city and already red leaves were falling and a cold wind blew off the gray sea. Kiku's residence resembled a fortress in its size and defenses, and was high on a slope on the northeast side of the city, with watchtowers that looked out to the north and the south, along the course of the river that linked Lake Kasumi to the sea. Beyond that, far in the distance, lay the capital, Chika said, adding he had never been there. Mu had flown above it, had seen its lord in his sickness, but he did not mention this.

The river cut a narrow valley through mountains that rose sheer from the shoreline, their peaks already white with snow. Its estuary formed the port, the only secure harbor on the Northern Sea. Whoever controlled Kitakami controlled trade with Shin and Silla, and the lands of the barbarians in the north. And, from the first impression of Kiku's home, it was clear to Mu who that was.

The imposing gates on the west side stood open, but he could see how they would close at a moment's notice, making the place impregnable. Guards stood in front of them, acknowledging Chika as they rode in. They all had some deformity: a missing eye, hand, or leg, twisted limbs, scarred features. Yet Mu was aware of hidden abilities that compensated for their handicaps.

Kinpoge had sat behind him most of the way, except when pain from the unfamiliar act of riding forced him to walk for a while, and she took the reins. She liked being in control of the horse and begged him not to lead her but to let her canter after Chika. Now she slid down from the gray's back and was immediately surrounded by a clutch of children of all ages, chattering at her, pelting her with questions.

A man came to lead the horses away, a couple of large dogs at his heels. He smiled shyly at Mu, who realized it was his youngest brother, Ku. They embraced, Ku awkward and seemingly embarrassed.

"You can talk later," Chika said. "I'm sure Ku is very busy and Kiku is waiting for you."

Mu raised his eyebrows, but Ku merely bowed deferentially without meeting his gaze. It was obvious that, as the tengu had told him, Kiku had made Ku his servant.

Chika urged him forward.

"Stay with your cousins," he told Kinpoge, who looked as if she was going to follow them. "They'll take you to meet your aunt Kaze. You'll meet your uncles later."

Apart from the men at the gate, Mu's sharp hearing told him others were concealed in the guardhouse, and when they were shown into Kiku's presence, he knew there were more, in alcoves and behind curtains around the room.

He is afraid I'll attack him! The idea amused him. He did not often need the cane to walk with, but he had brought it with him and now leaned on it, a little more than was necessary.

From the veranda they entered an anteroom where screen doors slid open silently to allow them into the main hall. It looked out over the cliffs to the sea, and the restless surge of the waves below was a constant background noise. On this bright autumn day the sea was calm, its color deep indigo. In the distance, several white-fringed islands could be seen. One had the red bird-perch gate of a shrine; the others seemed uninhabited except by seabirds. Twisted pines had been carved into grotesque shapes by the northeasterly wind. Mu tried to imagine what it would be like in winter, when snow covered the town and gales lashed the fortress.

The room was spacious, sparsely furnished, the floor dark polished cedar, the shutters cypress, their inner surfaces carved with scenes of life in Kitakami. One side was covered with woven wall hangings of exotic landscapes, dragons, and sea serpents.

Kiku sat at the far end, his back to the sea. The brightness of the light made it hard to see his face. On his right was his brother Kuro, on his left the warrior Tsunetomo, who had tied Mu up and left him crippled. Both Kuro and Tsunetomo had mustaches and beards, unkempt like wild men, but Kiku was clean shaven. Mu studied all three of them, glad to realize he felt nothing, no anger, no resentment.

Chika had entered the room after him and now went down on one knee, bowing his head low. Mu remained standing. To his surprise, both Kiku and Tsunetomo placed their hands palms down on the matting and, leaning forward, touched their foreheads to the floor. After a moment's hesitation, Kuro followed them.

Chika shuffled forward and indicated a silk cushion. Mu sat down, cross-legged. Kiku raised his head. Tsunetomo and Kuro stayed low.

"Welcome, brother," Kiku said. His voice had changed, had become deeper and more cultured, yet the same hard edge was still there and still menacing. His eyes were gleaming, but at the same time expressionless. His skin had lost its copper tone and was pale, as though he rarely went outside. "I am very glad to see you again. I believe our old friend Chika has conveyed to you my deep regret for the past."

Mu wondered how genuine he was and how much of it was part of some deep, elaborate scheme. What were his true intentions? At any moment, his brother might make a signal and the unseen guards would emerge and fall on him. He felt his right hand edge closer to the cane he had placed beside him. They might not be expecting to fight a man trained by a tengu.

The movement, slight as it was, did not escape Kiku. "I can understand that you don't trust us. We treated you very badly."

Kuro raised his head and said, "Not me. I wasn't there. I don't see why I should have to grovel."

Kiku made a gesture to silence him. "Those old rituals demand a high price. We have all paid it in different ways. But it was worth it. You will see the power I have drawn from the skull. Gessho was an extraordinary man."

"In other words, you would do the same thing again," Mu said, more amused than angry.

"Well, I suppose I would. I am glad we can be honest with each other. Tsunetomo, you may sit up now. My brother understands, and to understand is to forgive." He addressed Mu again. "Really, Tsunetomo has nothing to apologize for. He agreed to serve me, he was obeying me. Any offense was mine alone. But I thought you would like to see such a warrior prostrate before you. It is quite a pleasing sight, isn't it? I never tire of it. From now on, you and I are as one, in his eyes and the eyes of all his men. You only have to say the word and they will grovel at your feet. They will thrust their swords into their own throats if you command it."

"Why have you summoned me here?" Mu said.

"So we are reconciled?" Kiku exclaimed. "Come closer so I can embrace you."

"We needn't go that far," Mu returned.

"It's what people do!" Kiku's face was more animated now, as though he, too, found their situation amusing. "We embrace to show we are reconciled, and as long as one of us doesn't take advantage of the hug to stab the other in the back, we are friends, from now on, as brothers should be."

Mu began to laugh. He understood Kiku perfectly, as no one else ever would. He went forward and they embraced briefly. As he held the thin, wiry frame, so similar to his own, he felt he could read every thought that arose within his brother's mind.

"Let's drink!" Kiku clapped his hands to summon servants and wine.

After the first cups were filled and emptied, Kiku told Chika and Tsunetomo to leave, and take the guards with them. The wall hangings rippled as though a mild earthquake had struck, and an assortment of warriors poured out. Like the guards at the gate, many had limbs missing, a leg made from carved wood, a metal hook in place of a hand. Some had lost part of their skull and covered the wounds with a variety of masks, some had terrible scars or had suffered burns that left the skin seared white. Each made a reverent bow to Mu as they filed past him.

"That's just a small part of them," Kiku said. "Aren't they hideous? My crippled army. Hideous in the eyes of men but beautiful to me. I like looking at their scars and their injuries and contemplating their courage and their endurance, all now dedicated to my service."

"How do you do it?" Mu asked. He couldn't help admiring Kiku's effrontery.

"Men are not hard to manipulate," Kiku replied, pouring more wine into Mu's cup. "Especially warriors, who are so proud and so single-minded. Loyalty and courage are everything to them. Give them the opportunity to risk their lives a couple of times a month and they are happy."

"But who do they fight against?" Mu said, draining the cup and holding it out for a refill.

"That's a very good question. Now that we've wiped out the bandits on land and subdued the pirates at sea, we are running out of opponents. My cripples are getting restless. Their old wounds ache at night and remind them of ancient grudges. Cleaning up a pack of outlaws is all very well, but what they yearn for is the chance to confront those in whose service they got those injuries and who then disowned them: the Miboshi in Miyako, the Kakizuki in Rakuhara."

"You cannot take on both those forces," Mu said.

"I think I can," Kiku replied, "though it would be easier if I had a warrior as a figurehead and a cause."

Kuro laughed loudly and emptied his cup.

"The warrior would be Shikanoko," Mu said, after a pause, "and the cause the true emperor?"

"Exactly!"

"But . . . Shika has even more reason to hate you than I have. If it had not been for you, the Princess would not have died."

"That really was not my fault," Kiku said. "It was Kuro's snake."

"Well, I've lost count of how many times I've told you I was sorry," Kuro said sulkily.

"I know, I know," Kiku said. "But wait till Shikanoko

sees what we can offer him. The chance to fulfill his destiny, just as Chika's father dreamed."

"Is that what this is for?" Mu said. "You want to impress Shika and win his respect, and his gratitude?"

For the first time a vulnerable expression came over Kiku's face. "He is one of our fathers," he said. "He brought us up and taught us everything. Now that I have children of my own I understand what that means. I want to see him and thank him. What's wrong with that?"

"Shika has a son," Mu said. "A fully human boy, the child of the Princess. I am acquainted with him. He is a true warrior."

Kiku had gone pale. His hand as he refilled his cup trembled. "I did not know that," he murmured, and fell silent for a long time.

He is jealous, Mu thought. *He mocks people for their emotions, but he is no more immune to them than I was, and still am.* Then he wondered if Kiku's emotion was genuine, if he were not acting out something he had learned in order to hide his true motives. What did he truly want from Shika?

"You are deluding yourself if you think Shika is going to treat us as sons," he said. "If he does return it will be as a warrior, and no warrior family will admit to the taint of blood like ours, Old People from the Spider Tribe, born from cocoons."

Kiku leaned forward and spoke in a hiss. "I have made my own tribe. I can make or break the mightiest of warlords, even the Emperor. No one is safe from me and mine. My power is based on fear and on wealth—there are no forces stronger than these. Tell Shikanoko I will place all this at his service."

"You want me to find Shika in the Darkwood?"

"If you don't go I will send Chika, and the outcome may be very different."

"What do you mean?"

Kiku whispered, "Chika hates Shikanoko."

Mu was thinking of the vision he had seen when he flew above the land, as if it had been a scroll or a Go board. All the pieces were in their positions, and flames were charring the edges. It was time to act. It was his turn now to be a player and all his training had prepared him for this. The tengu had already told him what he was to do: *Join forces with your brother, find Shikanoko, and offer him these forces so the Emperor might be restored and Heaven placated.*

"I will go and find him," he said.

6

TAKEYOSHI

Take woke, the wind rushing against his face. He thought he was still asleep, for he often flew like this in his dreams. But this was many times more real and more vivid. Something gripped him firmly and painfully by the shoulders, the chill air brought tears to his eyes, and, though his vision was blurred, he could see enough to perceive below him the treetops, ranges, and rocky crags of the Darkwood.

He had no idea what had happened to him, and for a moment terror churned in his stomach. He had put all his trust in Kinpoge's father, setting aside his misgivings, above all his suspicions of the sorcery in which the hut was steeped, and accepting the casual spells that Mu and Kinpoge used daily, even though at times they made his skin crawl. He had learned to conquer his distaste and discern the magic, though he would never be able to use it himself. Now he feared Mu had betrayed him, had handed him over to some evil being, maybe like the snake woman he had met in the forest, or had himself been overcome in some epic struggle that he, Takeyoshi, had slept through and in which he was the prize.

He tried to banish his fear and assess the situation, as Mu had taught him.

I am alive, he thought, *but I have no weapons. The first thing I must do is arm myself.*

Blinking hard, he began to search the terrain below for something suitable. At the same time, he was noticing landmarks, trying to orient himself. It was early evening, the moon rising in the east, the evening star just over the jagged mountain peaks. They—he and whatever creature had him in its grip—were heading north. He could see the distinctive cone shape of Kuroyama, wreathed in white-steam clouds. In the west the sky was still pink and orange from the setting sun and the clouds flamed like dragons.

Was it a dragon that carried him? The wings that beat above his head, the gripping claws, suggested it might be. He tried to turn his head to look and caught a glimpse of blue cloth. Leggings? Surely no dragon ever wore leggings, blue or any other color.

A harsh, deep voice sounded in his ear. "Don't wriggle. I don't want to drop you!"

He caught a whiff of its smell, meaty, peppery. So it could speak, and it did not want to drop him?

The tops of the trees came closer. A flock of roosting green pigeons flew out, startled. Take drew up his knees instinctively as they cleared the canopy. The ground rushed up toward him. There was a huge beating of wings as the creature slowed and hovered. He felt it release its grip. He had already spotted the rock he was going to use. He rolled in a forward somersault, grabbed the rock, stood, gauged the distance, and threw, all in one rapid movement.

"Ow!" the creature exclaimed as the rock caught it in the chest. It reached over its shoulder and drew the long sword from the scabbard on its back. Take did not want to reveal how much the sword impressed him. Leaping backward, his eyes not leaving his opponent, he reached behind him for a branch he had noticed in his first forward roll. He picked it up and stood, taking in clearly, for the first time, the sight of the tengu—for he realized that was what it must be.

It looked furious. Its eyes were bulging, its shock of dirty white hair stood on end, and its wings thrashed above its head. He thought steam was even coming out of its nostrils, but possibly it was just its breath in the chill mountain air.

He gripped the branch more firmly, remembering Kinpoge's warning. *Be careful what you hope for.*

The sword came whistling down and cut the branch clean in half, sending a jarring pain through Take's right hand. He dropped the branch and jumped backward to avoid the sword's returning stroke.

"There," the tengu grunted. "I could have got you *there* and *there*." The sword struck out, and again, in the direction of Take's throat. "You're quick, though, that's good, and strong. I didn't expect you to be able to throw that rock so hard and so far. Now, shift your weight and come forward, under the blade. If you are unarmed, your hands and feet, even your head, must become weapons. Go for the soft parts, the eyes, the throat, the privates."

Take stood still, his breath panting. He held up his hands. "I'm sorry, I didn't mean to attack you. I didn't know who you were."

"And now you do?" the tengu said, amused.

"You are the tengu who taught my teacher," Take said. "And I hope you are going to teach me."

"Well, maybe I am. Yes, it looks like that's the way it's going to be." The tengu sheathed the sword. "You can call me Tadashii."

He opened his red jacket and inspected his hairy chest. "Look at that!" he exclaimed. "You gave me a bruise! I haven't had a bruise like that for a century or more. Oh, I am going to enjoy myself! But tell me, how did you get to be so strong?"

"I've been an acrobat all my life," Take replied. "I grew too tall to be a tumbler, but I've carried adult men on my shoulders, two or three at a time, for years."

"Hmm." Tadashii looked pleased. He took Take's hands and looked at them. "Great strength here, too. I suppose you can climb?"

"As well as any monkey," Take said.

Tadashii pointed at a pine that rose, bare trunked, about sixty or seventy feet tall. It was the last in a line of trees that stopped abruptly on the edge of an old lava flow.

"Climb that!"

Take went to it and shinned up, using his hands, clasped

behind the trunk, and his strong toes. When he got to the branches he continued to climb. Above him rose the huge mass, the cloud-fringed cone, of Kuroyama. There was a strong smell of sulfur, and steam rose from vents in the ground. It was how he imagined the entrance to hell. He could see Tadashii far below, and waved to him. Then, smelling smoke and hearing voices, he looked in the other direction. Beneath the sulfur was a rank odor of meat, and some animal scent, like a fox's den.

He could see down into a space between the trees where a group of creatures like Tadashii gathered around several large flat tree stumps. Torches lit their long noses, their beaks, their furled wings. He could hear the clack and rattle of stones.

The branches parted as Tadashii flew up to sit beside him.

"What are they doing?" Take whispered.

"They are playing Go," Tadashii replied. "I sometimes play myself." He waved his hand toward the edge of the clearing where a huge, long-nosed fellow sat hunched, contemplating the stump in front of him. "I have a game going on over there, but I've been waiting for what would seem like months, to you, for my opponent to make his move. He's always been a slow player. He's got himself into a bit of a pickle and he's trying to plan a way out. Still, we're some way from the endgame."

Kinpoge had been trying to teach Take to play Go, but he had not yet grasped its essence or its intricacies. Now, watching the tengu play under the moon and the torchlight, he was seized by a desire to learn to play properly.

"Will you teach me?" he said.

"If we have time," Tadashii replied. "Let's fly over their heads. I want him to see you. I think it will unsettle him."

His clawed hands and feet gripped Take's shoulders again and lifted him off the branch. Together they swooped low over the clearing, making several of the tengu look up. Some raised their arms in greeting, some muttered a welcome, but mostly they remained absorbed in their different games. Tadashii's opponent looked up with a scowl as Tadashii circled above him, showing Take off and cackling with laughter.

He shook his fist and bared his teeth at them before returning to his scrutiny of the board. Take glimpsed just enough to see that the grid was carved into the surface of the stump. The light showed bowls of white and black stones. Kinpoge played with seeds, pebbles, berries, on a board Ima had made for her.

"Back soon!" Tadashii called, as they soared over the trees to the place they had landed before. "He will take even longer to make up his mind now," he said, in a smug tone of voice.

"I don't quite understand what you are talking about," Take said, politely.

"Don't worry about it. One day you will, if you live that long. And I think you will, for I intend to make use of you. When it comes to the endgame. You may rest for a little while, until dawn. Would you rather sleep on the ground or in the tree? I myself will take that branch. I find it quite comfortable. Don't walk around in the night—there are pools of scalding water. It's dangerous."

Take looked at the ground beneath his feet. It was too dark to see clearly, but it seemed to be covered in stones, both large and small. Yoshi and Saru often slept in the crook of a branch, but he did not like it much, his legs being too long to fold up comfortably.

"I'll lean against the trunk," he said, and began to clear away some of the stones so he could sit down.

"You came rather unprepared," the tengu remarked, as he settled on his favorite branch.

"I didn't know I was coming," Take muttered. It was much colder high in the mountains and he had no covering. Mu's hut was far from luxurious, but at least there was no shortage of firewood, furs, and food. He was already hungry and thirsty and wondered when, if ever, they would eat or drink.

He did not really sleep, just dozed a little, waking with a start at every noise: the hiss and roar of the volcano, the wind in the trees, owls and other night birds, the distant howling of wolves. He had never felt so alone.

I could die here and no one would ever know. The tengu would probably crack my bones.

He had lived all his life among people, the noisy, milling world of the acrobats and the monkeys, yet he had always felt different from them. He had been removed from one world, but he was not yet in the next. He was determined that this time with the tengu would be the bridge between his old life and his new.

He shed a few tears of loneliness, since no one could see him, and then, with gritted teeth, he set himself to practice the meditation Mu had already taught him.

"Don't grit your teeth," the tengu told him next morning. "You are not lacking in strength—what you need is fluidity. At the moment you block your strength. You must learn to let it flow."

He had been boiling two large pale blue eggs in one of the steam vents. He took one egg and shelled it, hot as it was, sprinkled it with the salt that was encrusted on the rocks, and handed it to Take.

Take crammed it into his mouth, burning his tongue.

"And don't eat so quickly, you'll burn your mouth," Tadashii warned, too late.

The egg had been preserved in some way and tasted old, not exactly stale, but not fresh either, a little sulfurous. "Is there anything to drink?" Take said, when he could speak.

"I always forget how needy humans are," Tadashii said. "Suck a pebble. I'll find some water later." He shelled and ate the other egg, smacking his lips.

Take waited until the tengu had finished eating and then asked, "Why have you brought me here?"

"Your teacher, the Warrior of Nothingness, has had to go somewhere. I said I'd take care of you for a while. He sends you his regards, and says goodbye on his daughter's behalf."

"Kinpoge went with him?"

"You know, you will see Mu again, but not her."

The thought made Take sad. He missed her already.

The tengu looked at his face as if trying to read his expression and failing. "Well, never mind all that. Let's get to work! You're going to need a sword and a bow. You've probably seen the sword I made for Mu. I'll make one for you, once I've seen your reach and your stance. I already have a good idea of your strength."

He flew up and plucked a pole from where it was concealed in the lower branches of the tree.

"It's not a bad idea to keep a few weapons hidden in your castle," he observed, giving the pole to Take, "where you can reach them easily. Just a little advice for the future."

"I'm going to have a castle?" Take said, as he tested the heft of the pole, gripping it in both hands as Mu had shown him.

"Well, why not?" Tadashii replied, eyeing Take's hands but not making any comment, as he raised his sword. "I'd want a castle if I were you. Castles invoke respect from those above you and fear from those below. They keep your men occupied while building and give them somewhere to live when completed. I'll show you how to build a proper one out of rocks and stones."

A castle! Men! Then Take emptied his mind as they sparred for a while, the tengu setting a fierce pace but pulling his strokes before hitting either Take or the pole.

"That'll do for now," he said finally. "You can go and get your bow. Once that's done, we'll make the sword and some arrows."

When it was obvious he was not going to say any more, Take asked tentatively, "Are you going to tell me where the bow is?"

Tadashii jerked his head up. "There."

Take raised his eyes to the crags that marched in a jagged line up Kuroyama. The rock was black basalt, the ground old, pitted lava, covered with small, sharp stones. Here and there pools of sulfuric water and mud bubbled viscously, and steam hung around the slopes of the mountain. Beyond the tree he had climbed, broken trunks, like the spars of the wrecked ships that were exposed when Lake Kasumi dried up, showed where the fire and the sulfur had done their lethal work.

In the closest crag there was a narrow cleft, as if it had been split from top to bottom. Take squinted up to where the steam refracted the sunlight into rainbows, and for a moment thought he could see the shape of a giant bow.

"That's it," Tadashii said. "Ameyumi is its name. The Rain Bow."

"I am to climb up there for it?" Take moved a little closer, assessing the rocks and the cleft. The smooth basalt offered few footholds, but the cleft reminded him of the space, a yard or so wide, between the monkeys' shelter and the outer fence of their enclosure. The young males often played in it, inventing different ways to scale it: both feet on one side, rear on the other; one foot on each side, pushing up with the hands. It had to be done quickly, so the momentum itself carried you upward. It would be slippery from the steam and probably hot, too.

"You don't think you can do it?" Tadashii said, sounding disappointed.

"I didn't say I couldn't," Take replied, all the more determined. "I'm just working out the best way. But couldn't you just fly up and get it?"

"Not without attracting its owner's attention."

"It has an owner I have to steal it from?"

"In a manner of speaking. It's not really his, though. He won it in a wager from someone else, years ago, and *won* is a rather relative term, since he almost certainly cheated, so you could say he also stole it."

"Who from?"

"Some warrior who was fighting in the north and fancied himself an expert at Go." The tengu gave a smirk as if there was much more he might say but chose not to.

"Why is it up there?"

"Too many questions!" Tadashii cried. "Are you going to get it or not?"

"All right." Take went closer to the crevice, laid a hand on each side, and peered up. It was harder to see the bow now, the steam and the dazzle of light at the top obscured it, but he thought he could make out the arc of its shape. The surface under his palms was warm and slick. He tested it against the soles of his feet. They were rough, hardened from years of running around and climbing barefoot, and would not need covering, but he wanted to give his hands more protection.

He was still wearing the headband and short red jacket and leggings that all the acrobats dressed in. He retied the headband and took off the jacket, borrowed the tengu's knife to make the first cut, and tore off strips to bind around his palms.

He had noticed the night before that sticky resin oozed in places from the pine tree. He collected enough to rub into the balls of his feet and onto the bindings. The resin gathered a little sand and grit, which would give him extra grip.

He did not say any more to Tadashii. The preparations were helpful in themselves, but mostly they were to build up the inner impulse, the coiling of the spring that the acrobats used to launch themselves into impossible feats. He could feel it mounting within him, the desire to challenge the limits placed on the human body and the pull of the earth itself.

His first ascent was quick—feet, then hands, push upward, jump—but he had misjudged the distance. The bow was higher above the mouth of the crevice than he had expected. He could not reach it and, anyway, needed both hands to hold on to the slippery sides. He descended quickly in the same manner and rethought his strategy. He would have to continue his climb into one all-risking leap, and grasp the bow with both hands.

And then? He would slide down—or more likely fall. He would have to hold the bow upright, so he would not be able to use his hands to save himself. The best he could do was try to cushion the fall. He ran back to the pine, climbed to the first branches, and broke off as many needle-leafed twigs as he could carry. He spread these over the floor of the cleft.

"Hurry up!" Tadashii cried. There was an urgent tone in his voice, but Take did not want to be distracted now. Without replying, he took a deep breath and launched himself upward. The interior of the crevice seemed hotter and steamier. But he had reached the top once already, which gave him confidence. This time he went all the way to the lip, stood, reached up through the shimmering rainbows, felt the firm wood of the real bow, and grasped it. It resisted his hold and he needed both hands to pull it toward him.

Above him the volcano rumbled and hissed, and through the noise he heard another sound—a beating of wings, a cry of rage. The huge tengu that Tadashii had shown him the night before was flying toward him, clearly holding a drawn sword.

A premonition came to Take that one day he would fight this tengu—but now was not the time. Holding the bow close to his chest, he dropped down into the crevice.

He slid, fell, slid again, but somehow he and the bow stayed upright until he landed on the springy bed of pine. He had had many falls as an acrobat and knew how to roll out of them, but the crevice was narrow and he had to protect the bow. The shock jarred his spine and for a moment he feared he had broken an ankle. He was gasping for breath, the hot air burning his throat and lungs, but at the same time he was filled with excitement and elation.

He passed the bow through the narrow opening and slid out after it, tearing off the soaked bindings before they scalded his palms. Then he picked up the bow, marveling at its huge size and perfect balance, the intricacies of its bindings, its many layers of compressed wood. It seemed covered in a shiny substance that must have protected it from the steam, for, though old, it was unwarped and true.

"Well done!" Tadashii was at his side. "I think we might go somewhere a little quieter so you can practice with it and I'll get on with the sword."

The other tengu was screaming in rage from the top of the crag. A sudden hail of small rocks began to shower down on them. Take could not see if the tengu was throwing them or if the volcano was erupting. He gripped the bow more tightly as Tadashii picked him up and they flew back to the shelter of the Darkwood.

"They left for Kitakami," Ima said when the tengu brought Take back to the hut. The fire was a pile of glowing embers and a hare was roasting on it. Ban turned its head toward them in a strange questioning way.

"I know," Tadashii replied. "Takeyoshi and I have some work to do and then I am going to show you one or two things, too."

Ima raised one eyebrow but only said to Take, "You must be hungry."

Take realized he was, and very thirsty, too. He went to the stream and drank deeply, then splashed water on his face. He had placed the bow by the fire, and when he returned Ima had picked it up and was studying it.

"Is it Shikanoko's bow, Kodama?"

"It was his father's," replied the tengu. "Ameyumi is its name. What is Kodama?"

"Shisoku made it for Shikanoko. We were only children, but I remember it. And he reforged a broken sword, Jato."

"I don't know about Jato," Tadashii said, frowning. "Ameyumi was my concern. It was gained unfairly. Shikanoko's father staked his weapons, his own life, his son's, even the Emperor's. His opponent cheated and he lost everything. But in this new game, I'm going to win. Getting Ameyumi back was a major move."

"So it was my grandfather who played the game of Go and lost?" Take said, his voice breaking with excitement.

"That's correct," Tadashii said. "I thought it quite elegant to have you regain it."

"Are we going to give it to my father?" Take asked.

"Maybe. First I'll show you how to use it. It's good that you are already so strong. Then Ima and I will make you a sword."

Take opened his mouth, but before he could ask even one of the questions teeming in his mind, Tadashii said, "It's best if you just do as you're told for the time being."

"Can I ask a question?" Ima said, smiling at Take's expression.

"You most certainly may." Tadashii clapped Ima on the back.

"What do you plan to show me?"

"Someone has to take control here. You can't let this place just wind down and dwindle away. Everything Shisoku collected is still here. You have to learn how to use it and become the protector of the forest he was."

"Mu could do that," Ima replied. "Or Kiku or even Kuro. I think you'll find I have no aptitude. I can hunt; I can cook; I can forge. That's enough for me."

"I'm not giving you a choice," Tadashii said, irritated. "I'm telling you how it's going to be. I expect the human to be argumentative, but you should know better!"

7

TAMA

"You were received by the Emperor?" Lady Tama's eyes were narrowed and the tone of her voice was skeptical. She was trying to hide her annoyance with her husband. Masachika had returned to Matsutani, after weeks away, and had immediately thrown the household into a frenzy of activity with arrangements for the great hunt. Lord Aritomo himself was to attend. Tama did not mind this so much; she was used to entertaining lords and warriors of the highest rank, and the twin estates were prosperous and well managed, their fields overflowing with fresh produce, their storerooms packed with soy bean paste, rice, barley, and casks of wine. There were deep cellars where ice was preserved throughout the hot summers, and, even in the years of drought, the streams that flowed from the Darkwood never dried up. Farther into the mountains, at Kuromori, there were many natural hot springs, renowned for their healing properties.

Tama loved her land and was proud of the way she had improved it. She was excited at the prospect of displaying its riches to Lord Aritomo. But she was less thrilled by the young woman Masachika had brought with him and installed in one of the pavilions on the lake, which Tama had had rebuilt, never dreaming who would occupy it.

She was aware he must have had girls before. They were separated for long periods and men, of course, had their needs. But this was the first time he had brought one to Matsutani, wounding and insulting his wife. It aroused painful memories of Kiyoyori and the woman who had bewitched him, who she believed had burned to death in the former pavilion.

"She is just an entertainer," Masachika told her airily. "She'll supervise the musicians and she knows some acrobats whom I am arranging to have brought here for the amusement of Lord Aritomo. She has her lute with her— you must have heard her playing."

"It sounds like a stubborn instrument and often out of tune," Tama said. "Or maybe she doesn't have much talent."

She had longed for Masachika's return. Her body still ached for him, but when they were finally alone on the first night of his visit, his lovemaking had been perfunctory and had left her unsatisfied. Since then he had not come to her room, making one excuse after another: fears for her health, his own exhaustion, a fever.

Fever indeed! she thought. *Girl fever.*

Now he had come to her telling her they must speak in

absolute privacy. She had sent her women away and they were alone together in her room, she kneeling, he cross-legged. She had had the shutters closed; the light was dim. It was the ninth month but still very hot with the lingering heat that was the hardest to bear.

At first she found it hard to believe him and then she was alarmed. Was Masachika really thinking of betraying Aritomo, of taking his place? It seemed impossible that the Emperor and his mother would have such a scheme in mind and would suggest it to him. She felt he must have misunderstood, was endangering himself and her.

"Lady Natsue herself sent for me," Masachika said.

"What was . . . *he* . . . like?" she said, hardly daring even to speak of him.

"I did not set eyes on him. He remained behind the blinds. It seems he wanted to see me, to see for himself what kind of man I am."

"Who else was there?" Tama asked. "I imagine he would be surrounded by attendants, and some of them, at least, must keep Aritomo informed of everything the Imperial Household says and does. I hope you were discreet."

"Well, you know I am often beset by complaints from the Household. I was simply investigating one of them. My conversation with Lady Natsue was so veiled as to be barely comprehensible. To the Emperor, I said little beyond platitudes, to which he responded with a few lines of verse. He is quite a good poet, they say. His mother intimated that I might correspond with them in this way. Both of them are known to love poetry."

"But you know nothing about poetry," she exclaimed. "Have you ever written a poem?"

"One or two, in my youth. I thought you could do it for me."

"You still need me for some things, then?" she replied, both pleased and angered.

"I need you for everything," he said. "You know I am nothing without you."

"Then send the girl away."

"Is that what's bothering you? You can't think she is a rival in my affection for you?"

"You seem overfond of her," Tama said, embarrassed to admit her jealousy.

"I don't care for her at all. I will send her away, immediately after the hunt is over. She and the acrobats can go back to where they came from. We will give Lord Aritomo the finest days of his life, and if they turn out to be his last ones . . . everyone knows how sick he is even though no one admits it."

She stared at him coolly.

"Look what you have achieved here," he said. "Imagine what you could do with an entire country."

He knew exactly how to tempt her. "If we are to undertake this endeavor we must trust each other completely," Tama said. "No secrets, no lies must ever be between us."

"I hide nothing from you," he said, moving closer to embrace her.

"I love you, Masachika," she said. "I always have, even when I was married to your brother. But I will never forgive you if you lie to me. Let's go and swear by Sesshin's eyes that we will always be true to each other."

"We will," Masachika promised. "But first I must tell you another secret."

She pulled away from him a little, staring into his eyes. "A good secret or a bad one?"

"I don't know yet. I believe Kiyoyori's daughter is alive."

"Hina? It can't be true! You yourself told me she drowned."

"I am sure she is the woman I was sent to investigate in Aomizu—the one who was accused of poisoning Lady Fuji."

"I always feared that girl would end up poisoning someone, with all the potions and ointments she used to concoct," Tama said. The news that Hina might have been alive all these years disturbed her. Memories of her stepdaughter returned suddenly, assailing her with their clarity: the girl's pale, serious face; the eyes that lit up only for her father; the manuscripts she was always trying to decipher; her undeniable beauty.

"It is another reason Asagao has come with me. She and Hina, whom she knew as Yayoi, were close friends. I am hoping I can track Hina down through her. If it is true that Yoshimori is still alive, Hina must know where he is. She poisoned Fuji to silence her and has gone to warn Yoshimori. I am going to find her once the hunt is over and bring them both either to Lord Aritomo or to the Empress, whoever offers the greater reward."

Asagao! Now that she knew the girl musician's name, Tama disliked her even more. But if she was only a pawn in this greater plan she could tolerate her.

The eyes lay in their carved recess in the west gate, as bright as the day when they had been torn from Sesshin's head. For years they had watched over Matsutani as their owner had promised. The guardian spirits that had occupied the house and caused chaos and destruction after the earthquake had remained in the gateposts all that time. Tama visited them daily, bringing offerings of flowers, fruit, and rice cakes. In the summer she brought ice to cool them and in the winter lit fires in braziers and wrapped the posts in straw to keep them warm. On this hot afternoon, in early autumn, she brought the first persimmons of the season, their orange waxy skin smooth beneath her fingers, and branches of purple bush clover. Masachika carried a flask of rice wine and two bowls, for the spirits liked to share a drink with whoever visited them. No one ever saw them, but the bowls emptied mysteriously, between one moment and the next.

She thought Masachika looked uneasy and it troubled her further. They both knew the power of the eyes. They had wept together before them on more than one occasion. The spirits had not misbehaved for years, but then they had had no cause. She was under no illusion that they would not recognize falsehood.

Tama's attendant had brought a mat, which she spread in

the gateway. The entrance was paved with flat river stones, powdered with the dust that blew everywhere in the hot, dry wind. It covered their clothes and stung their eyes and throats.

Husband and wife knelt side by side. Tama divided her offerings and placed them equally before each gatepost. Masachika filled the wine bowls and they both drank. Then he refilled them and offered them to the spirits. Tama watched him carefully. He performed all his actions flawlessly, but he kept his head lowered as though he did not want to meet the gaze of the eyes.

She said in a low voice, "Master Sesshin, I mistreated you badly. I shall never cease to regret my rash action. I ask you to forgive me." Her face, which was turned upward, was streaked with tears.

"Hidarisama, Migisama," she went on. "I thank you for your diligence and devotion in protecting our home. Please always continue to do so. In your presence, I swear that I will always be true to my husband and I will support him in everything he does."

Masachika was silent for a few moments, making her fear he was going to refuse to speak, but eventually he said quietly but firmly, "I thank you for the protection you have given this place for years. I hope we will see no disturbances from you while Lord Aritomo is here. I think you know my devotion to my wife and I swear I will never betray her."

Yet despite his steady voice Tama was aware of his inner conflict. His fists were clenched, sweat formed on his brow.

She could do nothing but pray with all her heart that he was sincere. She was about to stand when a voice came from the left gatepost.

"Is it Matsutani lady?"

"Yes, with our offerings. Let's drink," the other spirit responded.

"Wait a moment. Who is with her?"

"Matsutani lord, so-called."

Tama whispered, "It's years since they have been heard. What can it mean?"

"It must be a special day," Masachika replied with forced light-heartedness. "It's a good omen. They are not saying anything bad, they are just recognizing us."

There was a faint burst of mocking laughter.

"But what if they misbehave while Lord Aritomo is here?" Tama stood, and led him away from the gateway. She stopped and studied his face with her intense gaze.

"They will behave themselves," Masachika replied. "What reason can they have not to? The eyes are in place. We are their masters now. They must obey us."

Tama had been whispering, but Masachika spoke more loudly. A bee came buzzing between them, making him flinch. It must have been attracted by the clover blossoms, Tama thought, and watched as it settled on one of them. It was an ordinary bee, nothing supernatural. Yet she feared it might be a sign.

"I am just going to speak to the musician for a moment," Masachika said as they walked toward the house.

Tama stopped and stared at him. Before she could speak

he said hurriedly, "Don't misunderstand me. I need to send for the acrobats; she will know where they are."

Tama watched with fury as he strode swiftly to the pavilion on the lake. When she turned back to the gate, the wine bowls were still full. She went back to check once or twice during the rest of the day, but the spirits would not drink.

8

MU

"Before you set out to find Shikanoko," Kiku said to Mu. "I have something to show you. I'm going to give you a little demonstration of how I've used the powers you and I have, to build our empire."

"And me," Kuro put in. "I have powers, too!"

"You do, my dear brother, ones of your own that are very useful." He looked from one brother to the other and smiled. "Kuro's children have inherited his talents and so have mine."

It was early evening, a few days after Mu had arrived in Kitakami. He was already preparing to leave again and had expected to have an early night to be on the road by dawn. Now it seemed Kiku had other plans. Mu was curious to see what he had in mind, but Kiku seemed content to sit and talk.

"Kinpoge, your daughter, is very skilled, too. I've already seen proof of that. Of course, her mother was a fox woman and had magic powers of her own. I'm sorry, I don't want to wound you by bringing up the past, but I feel it has given her something special, superior even to my eldest son, Juntaro. I propose they marry and we will see how their offspring turn out."

"Kinpoge is too young to marry," Mu said.

"She will soon be old enough," Kiku replied. "We are five brothers, not like anyone else. We must establish our five families, and arrange our children's marriages carefully, to preserve what we have been given. After the first generation, we will not mingle our blood with that of outsiders, unless there are sound reasons of policy. We must maintain our tribe."

Mu had noticed how often Kiku used this word, *tribe*. It amused him, but he liked it, too. He liked the feeling of belonging to a family and had no compunction in leaving Kinpoge here. He felt her future would be secure among people like her. Far better for her to marry Juntaro, when they were old enough, than to yearn for Take.

"I've no objections," he said, "but give her time to settle in before you mention the idea."

"They may not have much time," Kiku said. "We don't know how long their lives will be. Look how quickly we have grown and how fast we are aging."

Mu looked at his brother and saw the image of himself: the fine lines appearing on the skin, the gray hair at the temples. They had matured as fast as insects and now frailty was coming on them as swiftly. How brief a lifetime was!

Kiku was studying him. "How about you? Did you ever

take another woman? There are plenty here if you feel inclined."

Mu made no response, but Kiku's words and the talk of marriage had awakened something within him. Here, among families and children, he realized how lonely he had been, and how much lonelier he would be if Kinpoge left him. Since he would rather die than let Kiku find him a wife, he would have to find one himself. He had not considered such things for years, but now the idea did not seem displeasing. However, he changed the subject. "What do you propose to show me?"

Kiku shook his head slightly and grinned, as though he knew all that Mu had been thinking, but he did not comment. He said, "There is a merchant who has tried to compete with me for some time. His name is Unagi. Chika was employed by him, but Unagi became suspicious of him after a death in Aomizu. A pleasure woman, who was obstructing my wishes in several ways, died. One of the girls was suspected of murdering her and ran away. Unagi fancied she was special to him and wants to find her, prove her innocence, and marry her. He insulted Chika, accused him of lying, and dismissed him."

"So what are you going to do?"

"Stop his meddling, once and for all," Kiku said, smiling even more widely. "In fact, I will be dealing with several problems at once. I will rid myself of a rival, Chika will have some very pleasant moments of revenge, and our sister will be spared becoming the wife of a merchant."

"Our sister?" Mu said, not understanding.

"The woman who fled, who everyone knew as Yayoi, is Lord Kiyoyori's daughter, Hina. She has gone into the Darkwood to find Shikanoko. You are aware Kiyoyori was one of our fathers? Chika was acquainted with the lady when they were children. To tell you a secret, I believe he has feelings for her. Doesn't he deserve to have her? He will marry no one else and I don't like to see him lonely."

Mu stared at Kiku without saying anything. He had not expected to be going out to commit an assassination. It seemed like an unnecessary distraction from his more important mission. Despite the tengu's training and the sword he had been given he was yet to kill anyone. He was puzzled by his brother's words and felt there was much Kiku was keeping from him. He calmed his breath and emptied his mind in order to perceive the truth of the situation. Was Hina the woman who loved Shikanoko and would be able to remove the mask? Did both Kiku and Chika know this?

He had thought Kiku was going to show him the skull and demonstrate its power. He wondered where Kiku kept the sacred object that had been taken at such great cost and made powerful at a greater one to him, death, pain, betrayal, and loss all bound into it, along with ecstasy and lust. He realized he was longing to set eyes on it and dared to say, "Will you show me Gessho's skull?"

Kiku stared at him. "If you like. I thought you might not want to see it, that it might arouse painful memories, even though we have put all that behind us. Come, follow me. I'll prove to you that I have no secrets from you, that everything I have is yours."

He pulled aside the wall hangings, nodded to the two warriors who were on guard behind them, and pressed a carved boss that opened a sliding door. Stairs led down the outside of the fortress, fastened into the rock face on which it was built.

"Be careful," Kiku said. "The spray makes the steps slippery."

Below them the sea surged, gray, green, and white. The wind was numbingly cold even though it was not yet winter.

At the bottom of the steps a wooden grille, reinforced with iron, covered the entrance to a cellar. In the shelter of the rock Mu heard Kiku whistling through his teeth, and as if at a signal the grille was lifted aside by two more of the crippled warriors. He followed his brother inside.

Once they had moved away from the entrance it became very dark, but Kiku like Mu had the vision of a cat, and went forward without hesitating.

Following him, Mu became aware of some force that was pulling him toward itself. He stopped for a moment, to see if he could resist it. He felt he could, but he did not want to. It was both a physical attraction and a seductive, emotional one, offering everything he had ever wanted, unlimited power to exercise his will.

"Don't worry," Kiku said. "I won't let it absorb you."

It was a strange choice of words, but aptly described his misgivings.

"You feel its power?" Kiku asked. "You will be able to see it soon, for it shines, day and night."

No sooner had he spoken than Mu saw the glow in front of them, and then he saw the shape of the skull, the gem eyes, the mother-of-pearl teeth. For a moment he was transported back in time to when he had last seen it, and he felt again in his limbs the excruciating pain, and in his heart the immense sorrow. Then he recalled the tengu's teaching and made his will firm against the skull's power and felt it surrender and recede.

"It is beautiful, isn't it?" Kiku murmured. "That is why it needed the beauty of a woman in its making, as did Shikanoko's mask."

Mu looked at it and saw its beauty, dispassionately, and remembered he had loved Shida.

The skull floated upward as Kiku lifted it.

"How is it used?" Mu said.

"It is not used. It just *is*. Its power flows through me and into everything I do. Gessho must have been an extraordinary man. Only the mask comes close to this in power." Kiku's voice was reverent. "I have often wondered which would be the stronger."

He placed his lips on the cinnabar lips of the skull and stayed without moving or speaking for several minutes. The skull's glow pulsed slowly, lighting Kiku's rapt face.

"It nourishes me," he said, as he lowered it. "Every day it makes me stronger."

When they returned to the steps the wind had increased to a howl and they did not speak until they were inside again.

"You can tell Shika about the skull," Kiku said then, pouring a bowl of wine and handing it to Mu.

"You think he will be impressed?" Mu said, with a trace of sarcasm.

Kiku flushed slightly. "I want him to be with us. Maybe I want him to be free."

Mu was thinking about the tengu's words. The mask would be removed by a woman who truly loved Shikanoko. But if that woman was Hina, why did Kiku speak as if she was his to bestow on Chika?

He knew where Hina was—in the Darkwood not far from where the brothers had been born. Kinpoge had taken his message about Take to her. But should he tell Chika and his brother this? Kiku might have any number of motives for bringing Shikanoko back from the Darkwood—wanting to impress him, wanting to free him, wanting him at the head of his army—but to Mu the most obvious one was that he wanted to get his hands on the mask and its power.

"It's been a long time since I've done this myself," Kiku confessed, as they prepared for the night attack. "I've missed it. I usually dispatch Kuro, who has become a supreme assassin. He doesn't have many feelings, which is a help. Follow my lead. Whatever I do, do it, too."

They dressed in leggings and close-fitting tops of tightly woven hemp, dyed dark indigo, wrapped cloths of the same color around their faces so only their eyes were exposed, and took up various tools and weapons, leather garrottes, flasks of poison, thin sharp knives. Mu carried the sword the tengu had given him, and Chika also brought his sword.

"Unagi's sons are sword fighters," he said. "They like to think of themselves as warriors."

"We hope to kill their father without rousing the household," Kiku remarked mildly.

"Better to clean out the whole barrel and not let the young eels escape," Chika replied. "There's an old man, too. I'll take care of him. You do your thing and I'll do mine. I see no reason why you should have all the fun."

"I suppose you have earned it," Kiku said, with the strange tenderness he often displayed for Chika.

It was a dark night with no moon, the middle of the ninth month. Again Mu's eyes dilated like a cat's. Kiku's did the same. Chika kept close to them, stepping carefully in their footprints. Even the stars were dim, obscured by a low-hanging haze. Mist rose from the river as the air chilled in the hours before dawn. From the harbor came the sounds of water lapping against hulls and the creaking of boats as they shifted with the tide.

Unagi's house lay on the opposite bank. There was no bridge across the Kasumigawa; during the day narrow flatboats sculled across and back, but at this hour they were all moored on the bank, their owners and sailors asleep in the flimsy huts or in the boats themselves.

The men moved without a sound. As Chika went to untie one of the boats, a figure rose from a pile of ropes and sailcloth on it. Fuddled by sleep, he did not have time to call out before Chika leaped into the boat and had him by the throat, turning his face toward Kiku. His desperate eyes, wide open, bulging, searched for help and found Kiku's gaze. They seemed to register something, a mixture of surprise and relief, and then rolled back in the head, as the man went limp, just as Ku had in the forest all those years ago. *I must remember never to look Kiku in the eyes*, Mu thought.

Chika slid the sleeping body over the side of the boat, letting it go with barely a splash. Mu watched it drift away, rolling in the current, the face showing pale in the darkness.

"Live or die, there will not be a mark on him," Chika whispered in satisfaction. "He's known to drink too much."

Everything had been planned meticulously, Mu realized, from the drunkard's boat to the exact time of the tide, which carried them across the river without their having to use the oars. The boat nudged gently against the opposite bank. They stepped out and waded through the water, carrying their swords above their heads. Chika knew Unagi's house intimately. There was a dock where boats were berthed. Two men lay slumped on the boards.

Kiku breathed in Mu's ear, "Kuro was here earlier."

A little way up, a bamboo grid covered an arch through which water flowed into the garden of the residence. As Chika lifted the grid aside so they could pass through, Mu felt something brush against his legs. Fish, or maybe eels: the household must keep them here, alive and fresh.

The water lapped at a series of shallow steps, leading up to a kitchen. Ashes smoldered in a stone oven and he could smell soy and sesame oil. A small girl crouched on the highest step, her head on her knees. Mu feared she had been poisoned, too, but she stirred as they went past, muttering something in a dream, not waking.

Silently they entered the main rooms of the house. The smell changed to sandalwood, mixed with the odor of people. Mu could hear the soft rise and fall of their breath. From beyond the gate a dog barked. They froze for a few moments, but no one in the house wakened. If there were any more guards they were at the outer gate.

Here and there lamps flickered, giving Mu glimpses of the rooms as they went through them, each opening into the next. The wooden floors gleamed, wall hangings shone with patches of red. Along the southern side ran a wide veranda, but most of the shutters were closed.

From the middle of the house came the sound of snoring. Chika's teeth showed white as he grinned and mouthed *Unagi* to Mu. He slid open the final door and let Kiku go in first.

Kiku took on invisibility immediately and Mu copied him, as he had been told. He could just perceive his brother's faint outline approaching the sleeping man.

Unagi lay on his back, his head on a wooden headrest. Kiku's movements were so swift, Mu hardly followed them. For a moment he wondered why the merchant began to twist and kick, why he was making that strange muffled grunting. Then he saw the garrotte in his brother's hands. Unagi was a big man and it seemed impossible that Kiku should be able to hold him down, but Kiku's invisible hands were like iron and relentless.

There was a trickle of water, a foul smell, and Unagi's struggles ceased.

In the silence that followed came a rustling and an

intake of breath as the old man, Unagi's father, stirred. Mu saw the gleam of Chika's knife, heard the soft sigh as it entered flesh and the gurgle of blood.

Kiku slowly became visible again. Mu could see his expression as the lamps flared. It was both stern and gentle, as if he had undergone a spiritual transformation. He smiled at Chika with that unfathomable emotion.

"That was for you."

Chika smiled back, pulled one of the hangings from the wall, and placed a corner of it against the flame. As it began to smoulder he lifted the shutter open; the breeze fanned the sparks into fire.

Jumping from the veranda, they ran across the garden to the main gate. A woman screamed from the house behind them. Shouts followed, pounding feet, the crashing of doors and shutters as they were flung open, the ever fiercer crackling of flames.

Kiku leaped for the top of the wall, scaling it easily, and Mu, still invisible, was right behind him, but Chika had turned back and drawn his sword. Running figures came from the guardhouse at the gate, their own swords glinting through the mist.

Two young men, barely into their twenties, came at Chika, attacking without hesitation. In the dark it was impossible to see their faces clearly, but their build and movements were so similar they had to be brothers. They possessed both courage and skill and Chika was forced back to the foot of the wall.

"Go and help him," Kiku ordered.

There was no time to argue, to plead that he had

nothing against these young men and no reason to take their lives. Mu dropped down beside Chika, letting visibility return, surprising the man on his left. The tengu's sword swung once and cut clean through his opponent's forearm. The other sword fell in a shower of blood, startlingly warm in the dawn chill.

With a cry of rage and pain, the man drew a knife with his left hand and stabbed at where Mu would have been, if he had not used the second self to avoid the blade, letting it pierce only his shadow. The man stumbled, and with a returning stroke, the tengu's sword cut him across the side of the neck, severing the artery.

Jumping over the dying man as he crumpled to the ground, Mu turned his attention to Chika. He became one person, fully visible. The surviving brother caught sight of him out of the corner of his eye and thrust at him. Mu made one of the lightning-fast feints the tengu had taught him.

"Leave him!" Chika cried. "This one is mine!"

Mu took a light step back, as the man swung at him again. He could have killed him then, but he heeded Chika's command.

"Your brother's dead," Chika shouted. "Your father, too! Go and join them!"

Unsettled, enraged, his opponent hurled himself forward. Chika's sword tip found his throat.

Kiku gave a cry of appreciation. Mu could see him. Day was breaking.

"Let's go!" Chika said to Mu and, side by side, they leaped onto the wall. All three dropped soundlessly down to the other side. They did not go back to the boat but ran swiftly away from the house, which was now ablaze, through the narrow streets, following the river upstream. By the time the sun rose they were walking along a high dike that separated the rice fields from the river. They strolled in a leisurely way, as though they had risen early to enjoy the autumn morning air. Eventually, they came to a pier jutting out over the water. The mudbanks were exposed by the low tide, and herons and plovers patrolled the shoreline, feeding. Under the pier, Kuro was waiting in a small boat, similar to the one they had crossed over in.

They did not speak as they climbed aboard. Kiku went first, followed by Mu. Chika handed his sword to Mu and pushed the boat into deeper water, then jumped nimbly in and took up the scull. His face was calm, almost rapt, as though some deep need had been fulfilled.

When they disembarked at the opposite bank, Kuro fastened the boat and looked up with an expectant expression.

"Well? How was it? Success?"

"Unagi and his sons are dead," Kiku replied. "His father, too."

"Well done! By what method?"

"Garrotte and swords," Chika replied. "We set fire to the house."

"I saw that." Kuro looked downstream to where the smoke was rising. "I still think poison would have been better."

"It depends on whether you want to send a clear message or not," Kiku replied. "With poison, or with snake or scorpion, there is always an element of uncertainty. This time there will be no doubt. The house of Unagi is finished and the same fate awaits all our competitors unless they submit to us."

As they walked back into the town the smell of fish being grilled for the first meal of the day wafted through the streets, mingled with the sweet odors of soy bean paste and curds.

"I'm hungry," Chika said.

"We can eat here." Kiku stopped in front of a low-roofed building whose back room had been extended over the river and turned into an eating place. A large cheerful woman was gutting fish that still quivered with life. She called out a greeting to them as they entered.

"Master Kikuta! What an honor! Welcome!"

They sat down on cushions, a low table between them. The breeze from the river smelled of salt and smoke. A young girl, so shy she did not once raise her head, brought sharp green tea and set the bowls before them.

"What a shame it is not the season. I feel like eating eel!" Chika remarked, making Kuro chuckle.

"Wasn't that fun?" Kiku said to Mu.

Fun? It had been shocking and elating. It had demanded a new level of single-mindedness and concentration. For the first time he had combined the tengu's training and his own talents. It made him feel alive and reckless, aware of his own physicality in a way he had not felt since Shida. But four people he did not know and with whom he had no quarrel were dead.

"I suppose it was," he admitted. "I haven't used the sword in a real fight before."

"You fight well," Chika said. "Not that I needed your help—I'd have dealt with them both alone."

Mu allowed himself the slightest smile of mockery but did not speak.

"Now that you've seen for yourself what we can do, you can tell Shikanoko," Kiku said. "No one is safe from us, no matter how cautious or how heavily guarded. Give him this." He placed a small piece of carved jade in front of Mu: a fawn in a bed of grass.

"Where did you get that?" Mu said, taking it up and caressing it with his fingers.

"It was among Akuzenji's treasures. I kept it because it reminded me of Shika. Whoever he wants to get rid of, we will do it. Tell him that, tell him we are his to command."

But beneath the words, in spite of the gift, Mu sensed his brother's lust for power.

9

BARA

Shikanoko had spent years in the north, living with men who chased narwhal through stormy seas and hunted seals on rocky shores. Sometimes they treated him as a god, for he had many powers that he made useful to them, and sometimes as an idiot, for he knew nothing of boats and fishing, and could not understand their speech, so they had to repeat everything three times or more. Then, like the migratory birds that came and went, summer and winter—the local people believed they were crabs that transformed into birds and then back into crabs when it turned cold—instinct told him it was time to take flight.

The Burnt Twins and Ibara followed him, as they had done for years. After a journey of several weeks they found themselves back in the old hut on the borders of the Snow Country.

One morning, Ibara thought she saw a stranger on the

edge of the clearing, but it must have been a trick of the light, for when she looked again there was no one. Still, she told Nagatomo and they began to notice signs: Gen, the fake wolf, howled at night; the deer were more nervous; there were footprints, smaller than any of theirs, around the pools. She felt she was being watched and began to take her sword with her when she went away from the hut.

When the figure finally came through the forest one evening while they sat around the fire, Nagatomo said, "It is Takauji," and Ibara recognized the young man, who had been no more than a boy the last time they had seen him.

"I realized you had come back," Takauji said, kneeling before Shikanoko and holding out his sword. "I came to offer you this. The Lord of the Snow Country will serve you loyally with all his men." Then he added less formally, "And if you are going to the capital take me with you, for I want to kill Aritomo."

"What makes you think I am going to the capital?" Shika said. "Maybe I will just stay here in the Darkwood."

Takauji scowled, saying forcefully, "My right to my land is still being disputed on the grounds my father was a traitor. Every year some new claimant tries to take the domain from me. I am tired of these challenges, of fighting skirmish after skirmish. They are provoked from Minatogura. I will never have any peace unless I control that city or Aritomo is dead—preferably both! I hoped you would support me."

"What does your mother advise?" Shika asked.

"She died last winter." Takauji suddenly looked much

older than his years. "But before she died she revealed to me my father's final words. No one dared repeat them, but one of his men had told her in secret: *Yoshimori is the true emperor* is what he said before he ripped his belly open. People say the true emperor will return, but he will never reign unless Aritomo is dead."

"Once, a long time ago, I made a vow," Shika said. "That I would find Yoshimori and restore him to the throne. But then the mask became fused to my face and I felt I was condemned to live out my life outside human society, like an animal in the forest."

"But even masked you can achieve great things," Takauji said. "Look how you helped me and my mother before. I would be dead by now without you."

Nagatomo leaned forward and spoke seriously to the young man. "Everything you desire must be fought for. And once it is won it has to be defended. You are young, it's true, but you are a warrior. Act like one."

"I will," Takauji promised, his face lightening.

Ibara felt Nagatomo's words had been directed at Shikanoko as much as Takauji. Shikanoko made no outward response, neither encouraging Takauji nor rebuffing him.

After that the young man came every few days to talk to them. Ibara could see that Shikanoko welcomed his visits. They must have made her careless, for the next visitor took her by surprise. Even though she carried her sword it was no use to her when the stranger let her see him, for he used some kind of magic to paralyze her arm. He appeared on the path in front of her, coming out of nowhere, and she had hardly drawn the sword before it slipped from her useless fingers.

"Don't be afraid," he said. "I don't want to hurt you."

She went for her knife with her left hand, surprising him, but when she lunged at the figure before her the blade struck empty air. His voice came from behind her and as she whirled around she lost all feeling in her left hand and the knife fell beside the sword.

"Gen!" she called, for the wolf had come with her.

"Gen," the man repeated, a note of delight in his voice. The wolf came bounding out of the undergrowth, sniffed the air, and then approached the stranger, its ears flat, its tail wagging.

"Gen," he said, stroking its head. "You're still alive? Do you remember me? Mu?"

"Gen knows you?" Ibara said wonderingly. "Where have you come from?"

"I've been sent to find Shikanoko. It's an added pleasure to meet a beautiful woman." The compliment sounded awkward, as if he were not used to making them. Or was it just that she was not used to hearing them?

"I have never been beautiful and I am hardly a woman anymore," she replied. "I live like a man and I can fight like a man, unless people use cowardly magic tricks!"

"I fight like a tengu," he said, laughing. "For that's who taught me. And it's by the tengu's command that I've come for Shikanoko. Let's go and find him. Unless you feel like doing something else first?"

"No, I certainly don't! Release my hands so I can slap your face!"

Mu picked up her weapons and she felt her hands return to normal. He came closer and thrust his face toward hers. He was thin and ordinary-looking, not very tall, of slight, wiry build, with rather small feet. His features were regular, his black eyes gleamed, his skin was copper-colored, beginning to show signs of aging.

"A slap is better than a kiss to a tengu," he said and laughed again.

It seemed a long time since she had heard laughter. She gave him a slap that made him stagger; in some ways it was as intimate as a kiss.

"What business do you have with the lord?" she said.

"Apart from anything else, I've come to pay him my respects. He is my father."

"Don't talk nonsense," she said. "He is no older than you."

"My brothers and I age fast," Mu said.

"Is that a tengu thing?"

"It's the opposite. Tengu age very slowly, and if they die at all, it's after hundreds of years. Presumably my life will be short. That's why I must never waste a moment or an opportunity." He raised an eyebrow at her.

He intrigued and repelled her in equal measure.

Nagatomo and Eisei were waiting with drawn swords. Mu halted and bowed deeply. "The Burnt Twins," he said. "I am honored to meet you. Your fame is widespread."

"Hand over your weapons," Nagatomo replied, unmoved by the flattery.

"I could give you my sword, but my true weapons are not the sort that can be handed over. But I have not come to hurt any of you, least of all Shikanoko." He looked around. "Where is he?"

"In the forest," Nagatomo said.

"Then I will wait for him." Mu perched his bony behind on one of the boulders in front of the wooden hut and grinned up at Ibara.

"Come and sit next to me and tell me the story of your life."

Her palm still tingled. "There is nothing to tell."

"Well, get me something to drink, then."

"Get it yourself," she replied, her own rudeness delighting her.

"We drink only water," Eisei remarked.

"In that case it's lucky I brought my own liquor."

From a pouch at his waist he produced a small bamboo flask, removed the stopper, and held it out to them. The two men declined, but Ibara grabbed it and took a sip and then, as all her senses welcomed the fiery liquid, another, deeper gulp.

"Ha! You've missed that!"

The last time she had tasted alcohol, Saburo had been alive.

She handed the flask back to Mu and he raised it. "To the dead!" he said, mocking and serious at the same time.

Gen turned his head and whimpered. When they followed his gaze, they saw Shikanoko on the edge of the clearing. Mu rose to his feet, taking a swig of liquor and handing the flask back to Ibara. She watched as the two men approached each other. They seemed about the same age. Shikanoko was the taller by a head, even without the antlered mask. Mu's demeanor was humble, and he dropped to his knees and lowered his forehead to the ground.

The lord hesitated for a moment and looked around. Then he stepped past the kneeling man as if deliberately ignoring him and continued walking toward the others. Gen ran, in his stiff awkward way, to Shikanoko's side, licked his hand, and then went to Mu, barking anxiously like a dog.

Shikanoko turned and went back. He knelt in front of Mu and taking him by the shoulders drew him into an embrace.

Ibara drank quickly, taking no notice of Eisei's disapproving glance.

The horses, grazing in the clearing, raised their heads to watch. Tan walked with an inquisitive air toward the stranger.

Shikanoko said something to Mu that Ibara could not hear, but it made him stop dead and look at the horse. She heard his laughter as Tan sniffed him. Mu sniffed back; they breathed into each other's nostrils.

It calms a horse, Saburo had said, long ago. Tears sprang into her eyes.

"I suppose I had better prepare some food," she said to hide them.

There was a rabbit, caught two days before, pods of wild beans, a little dried fish, burdock and other mountain vegetables. All through the meal she watched Mu. Usually they shared the cooking among the three of them, but the arrival of the stranger had somehow turned her into a woman again and she undertook women's tasks like she used to. She was annoyed and beguiled.

The food was sparse, the meal quickly over. The sun slipped behind the western mountains and the shadows turned mauve. The air cooled slightly. Frogs croaked from the stream and night insects began to call. Mosquitoes whined around their necks and Nagatomo threw green twigs on the fire to make it smoke.

Mu said, "Things cannot go on as they are."

"It is not my fault that Heaven is enraged," Shikanoko replied.

"But it is in your power to restore."

"Restore what? The Kakizuki are in exile. The Miboshi rule the whole country. Their choice of emperor sits on the Lotus Throne. I have nothing."

"Lord Kiyoyori is at your side and you have his sword, Jato, reforged for you. You have the Burnt Twins, and, in this woman, the instrument of Masachika's death. You have your son, Takeyoshi, who is becoming a fine warrior. I have taught him myself, so I know what I'm talking about. You have the true emperor."

"Yoshimori? I most certainly do not! I have no idea where he is."

"But I know," Mu said with a smile. "And that is why I have been sent to get you. He is with Lady Hina. I will take you to them."

Ibara's blood rushed through her veins and her whole

body tingled. *The instrument of Masachika's death! And Hina! Hina is alive!*

Mu gave her a grin as if he read her thoughts and then continued, to Shika, "And you have my brother Kiku, who has wealth, power, and an army of his own, which he has promised are all yours to command. He sent this as a sign." He took the jade carving from the breast of his robe and held it out.

Shika took it, gazing on it in wonder.

"It was in Akuzenji's hoard. Kiku kept it for you."

"I am surprised," Shika said slowly. "He must have changed.".

"He has. In some ways for the better, in some for the worse. Do you remember Gessho?"

Shika nodded. "But what does Gessho have to do with Kiku?"

"Kiku turned his skull into an object of power. It has made him almost invincible."

A long silence followed. Neither man moved until Tan neighed shrilly from the darkness and Shikanoko turned his head as if he was listening to a message.

"I would come," he said finally. "If I could come as a man. But I cannot appear before the Emperor as this creature, half stag."

His hands went to his face. His fingers touched the smooth bone.

"Remove the mask, Mu, and I will accompany you."

"It can be removed only by someone who loves you," Mu said, after a pause. "I'm not saying I don't love you. I think

I do. But I can't take the mask from you, and nor, I think, can any of us here."

"Do you think we haven't tried?" Nagatomo said out of the darkness.

Shikanoko laughed bitterly. "I destroyed my one chance of love."

"We never do that," Ibara said. "We are always given another chance." Mu looked over the flames at her and she hoped he didn't think she was talking about him. Then she hoped he did.

"I believe I know who can remove the mask," Mu said.

Tan walked up and put his head over Shikanoko's shoulder, rubbing against him. He stroked the horse's face.

Ibara said boldly, "It looks like Tan is telling you what to do."

"Maybe he is," Shikanoko said. "I will know in the morning."

10

SHIKANOKO

He went away from the fire toward the small clearing by the spring. The long grass was dry and dead. Ragged holes showed where deer had been digging to get at the roots. The spring's babble was muted. It had not rained all summer and whatever source fed the spring was drying up. He knew they could not remain there without water. It was one more reason to leave with Mu. If Yoshimori came to the throne would the drought end and the land recover?

The others had fallen silent. Maybe they were asleep, though he knew they would take turns in keeping watch, as they had done for years. They had sacrificed their own lives to stay with him, they had kept him alive, nourished him with their friendship.

What did I do to deserve that? What am I?

He felt the mask as he had done earlier, let his fingers caress the bone of the deer's skull, touched the lips, longed with all his heart to be free of it.

Should I stay here and die in the forest? But then I condemn those who have been loyal to me to the same endless exile.

Apart from the stags who cried in loneliness and yearning, the autumn forest had been emptying of sound. Birds flew south, insects chirped their final songs and buried themselves in the ground, or died. Scarlet and gold leaves covered the ground, rustling and dancing when the wind scattered them. Pine cones fell with a thump, and beech mast lay thick under the bare trees.

An owl hooted. Shika could feel the frost taking hold. He pulled the bearskin around his shoulders. How long was it since Nagatomo had killed it? The years merged into one another. Had he been away for ten winters or a hundred?

He thought about all Mu had told him. First his son, who had had to grow up alone, just as he had. When he had first met Ibara, he had told her, *Better he died in the water than grow up in this world of sorrow.* But the boy had somehow raised himself, had managed to find Mu and learn the way of the bow and the sword. He imagined him like Takauji, a young warrior.

An unfamiliar feeling came over him, stimulating and intense. After a few moments he identified it as curiosity. He said the boy's name aloud, listening to how it sounded: *Takeyoshi.* He wanted to discover how he had turned out, he wanted to look in his face and see whom he resembled. Takeyoshi could not escape the fact that he was a warrior, the son of a princess.

Next Akihime came into his mind, as strongly as if she stood before him. He thought he heard her say, "It was not you who killed me or caused my death. We disobeyed the gods; we were punished for it. Masachika took me prisoner, Aritomo ordered my torture, the Prince Abbot carried it out. Punish them if you will, but don't punish yourself any longer. I was dying before the serpent bit me—maybe it saved me days of suffering. And although what we did together was wrong—we were so young, we knew nothing about the world—our son came from it."

He recalled Sesshin's words: *This is why you should never concern yourself over your fate; everything follows the laws of destiny and therefore happens for a purpose.*

He saw all his faults and mistakes, his temper, impulsiveness, greed, and pride.

He had carried her memory in his heart, day and night, for years, and yet he had hardly known her and now he could not see her face, only her defiant stance as she faced him on the road. And at that moment he finally accepted that he would never see her again. His grief had run its course. *Farewell,* he said, *I will find our son.* Then he turned his thoughts to the other children whom he had tried to bring up, the ones Sesshin had warned him about. He had spared them, he must accept the consequences. He stroked the carved fawn, feeling its smooth jade surface. The gift touched him. He wanted to see Kiku and his brothers again.

Mu had told him that Kiku had gained his extreme power from the skull of the monk Gessho. Shika let this idea come into his mind and contemplated it for a long time. He slowly became aware of the power spreading out from Kitakami, seeking ever greater control and domination. He had ignored Kiku and the others for too long. His own spiritual power, honed by the years of solitude and denial, stirred in response, stronger than ever.

A little way from him, the horses moved and stamped, restless in the cold, their silver coats gleaming faintly in the starlight, their breath floating in small clouds. Sparks from the fire flew upward. Shika heard a low murmur of voices as Ibara took over the watch from Eisei.

He thought about the horses' lives, so entwined with his own, first Risu, then Nyorin, whom he had acquired after Akuzenji's execution. He had wept when Risu died, both for her and for the boy he had been when she came into his life. And then the other stallion, Tan, who carried the spirit of Lord Kiyoyori within him. Shika might have died with Akuzenji and all the other bandits, but Kiyoyori had spared him. Had he repaid that debt or did he still owe Kiyoyori his life?

He recalled his own voice saying, *She is in love with Nyorin. I think she will have a foal next year,* and a girl's voice replied, *I wish I could live with you and Risu and Nyorin and their foal. Why don't we get married when I am old enough?*

Hina had loved him then. She must have saved his son, kept him hidden for years. He should at least thank her for that. And he should take Tan to her, so father and daughter could be reunited. He dared not hope for anything more.

He could no longer ignore the truth: Heaven would not relinquish its stubborn desire to see Yoshimori restored to the Lotus Throne. And Shika could only bow to its will and accept that he was its instrument. He had within his grasp everything he needed for victory in that cause, and for his own revenge. He remembered Kongyo's dream so many years ago.

I saw you as tall as a giant, Kongyo had said. *Your head rested on the mountains of the north and your feet on the southern islands. I woke convinced Heaven has a plan for you. Why else should you have escaped death so many times?*

Kongyo was dead, but his words remained. Then he heard Nagatomo's voice as if he had spoken directly to him: *You are a warrior. Act like one.*

Finally, as if in a dream, Shisoku's words came back to him: *When you have mastered the dance you will gain knowledge through the mask. You will know all the events of the world, you will see the future in dreams, and all your wishes will be granted.*

The great power he had been promised hardly interested Shika, except insofar as he would use it to control and contain Kiku, while bringing Yoshimori to the throne. In that case, it did not matter if he was condemned to wear the mask forever. He would crush the Emperor's enemies and then retire again to the forest.

The night passed. He did not sleep. Just before dawn he saw eyes shining around the edge of the clearing. The deer had come to graze. He stood and moved among them. They did not startle but circled him as he danced, for the last time, the deer dance in the Darkwood.

One by one the others woke and came to join him. As the light strengthened he saw Takauji was among them. The young man must have known the movements of the deer dance since childhood. Shikanoko followed him in the autumn part of the dance, mastering the final ritual that he had never known. In the circling, interweaving patterns he saw his whole life and the part each of them had played in it, and the part he had played in theirs.

When the dance was finished, he called Takauji to him and said formally, "I accept the service you offered me."

Takauji's face lit up as he fell to his knees.

"I am going to Miyako," Shika said. "I am relying on you. You must hold the Snow Country for the Emperor."

"I will do more than that," Takauji promised. "I will take Minatogura!"

11

HINA

The acrobats had caught two suitable young male monkeys and were preparing to go back to Aomizu, but they were reluctant to leave without Take. The strange girl had come, in the eighth month, to tell the lady that he was staying with her father, but since then there had been no other messages, nor had Take returned.

Hina did not know whether she should leave with them or stay. The images of the face in the mask and the skull had never left her mind, but they did not reappear in Sesshin's book, and despite her daily study of it, along with fasting and meditation, no other sign was revealed.

The captive monkeys screamed all night and their families hovered anxiously in the surrounding trees, crying in forlorn voices. Hina felt like adding her own voice to theirs. *Come back, Take! Where are you? Come back!*

One morning she heard the sound of men's voices, and

went swiftly to hide herself behind the rocks around the hot spring. The pack horse raised its head from the grass and neighed in welcome.

She caught sight of a splash of red through the trees. Yoshi dropped down from the branch where he had been sitting, chewing on a twig and playing with Noboru.

"It's Kinmaru and Monmaru!"

Saru was soaking in the hot water. He leaped out naked and ran to the two men who were walking into the clearing. "What's happened?" he called. "Why are you here? What's wrong?"

The older men still behaved like children, Hina thought, and from a distance they still looked childlike, but when she approached she saw that the sudden aging common to acrobats had fallen on them. Their joints had succumbed to the demands made on them over the years, their faces were lined, they moved like old men.

"Lady Yayoi," Kinmaru said, and Monmaru bowed his head, yet she sensed a reserve in them toward her. She wondered what accusations had been made of her in her absence. Had they been sent to bring her back to be punished for murder?

"A message came from Lady Asagao," Monmaru began immediately, not even waiting to sit down. "She was taken to Matsutani by Lord Masachika. She must have made a good impression; maybe she spoke on our behalf. Anyway, the lord has summoned us, with the musicians, to entertain a great assembly, including Lord Aritomo himself, at a hunt in the southern Darkwood. Saru, you, and Yoshi must go with us. We are halfway to Matsutani, there is no point in going home first. The others will meet us there. They've already set out with the monkeys and all our equipment."

"It's a great honor," Kinmaru said. "And we will be richly rewarded, Asagao says. These lords know how to give generously. But we must leave at once, we have less than half a month."

"What about them?" Yoshi said, indicating the captive monkeys.

"You'll have to let them go," Kinmaru said. "We can't risk taking young, untrained monkeys with us."

Saru looked upset. "Then we've wasted the whole summer here. These are really promising ones, too."

"You can come back next year," Monmaru consoled him. "This is too good an opportunity to miss."

"Yoshi should take the young monkeys home with the horse," Hina said. She had been listening to the conversation with mounting dread.

They all stared at her. "We can't perform without Yoshi," Saru said.

"Where's Take?" Kinmaru looked around. "He'll need to come, too."

"He's gone off somewhere," Saru replied. "We can manage without him, but that's all the more reason why Yoshi must come."

He flung an arm around his friend's shoulder and hugged him. "Exciting, isn't it?"

"Yoshi," Hina said. "I need to talk to you alone."

Yoshi shrugged his shoulders slightly. His usually cheerful expression turned sullen as he followed Hina. Kon swooped overhead, calling piercingly.

Yoshi looked up. "I hate that bird," he muttered. "I wish it would go away."

When they were out of earshot, Hina said, "You must not go. You will be in great danger."

He made no response, just stared at the ground.

"Yoshi! Look at me! Do you understand what I am saying?"

He looked at her then, his expression unreadable.

"Do you remember anything about the past, where you came from, who you are?"

"I am an acrobat. I work with monkeys. That's the only life I've ever known."

Hina wondered if she should tell him: Would he be safer if he knew or would ignorance protect him?

Yoshi said, in a low, rapid voice, "I do remember one thing. A woman telling me I must never reveal my true identity. Kai knows, for she came with me from the same world, but she has never said a word to anyone else. That's why I love her and why she's the only person I could love. I know why Kon follows me day and night. I saw how Take's attitude changed toward me—you told him, didn't you? You have known since the day we met, for the lute betrayed me. I'm grateful to you for keeping my secret all these years. But I will never admit it to anyone. You can't make me. I will deny it to the end of my days. I am not interested in power or position. I will live and die an acrobat and nothing you can say will make me change my mind."

Even as he denied it he spoke with all the true authority of the Emperor. She found she could not argue with him.

The young monkeys were released, and were greeted by their families with cries of relief and excitement.

"You'll come with us, Lady Yayoi?" Kinmaru said, when they were ready to leave.

"I will wait for Take," she replied. "He will be back soon."

Monmaru said nervously, "We were told to bring you back with us. We will certainly be questioned about you."

"You must say nothing!" Yoshi declared and then, taking Yayoi aside, said quietly, "I promise I will not give you away, and you must make the same promise to me."

"I will," she whispered.

They did not try to persuade her further, fully aware she faced arrest if she was found. Better to starve to death in the Darkwood or be killed by wild animals than fall into the hands of Aritomo's torturers.

The monkeys disappeared. After the two young ones were released and the excitement had died down, they all began to hurry away to the northeast, deep into the forest, as if each member of the group had received a hidden signal.

Hina missed their chatter and their activity. The trees seemed to press around her more densely and she heard strange noises that alarmed her. Kon had flown after Yoshi, adding to her fears—surely Masachika or one of his men would have the skill to shoot the bird down? Yet there was no way she could prevent him from following Yoshi, just as she could not stop Yoshi from going to Matsutani. He was the Emperor, he would go where he willed and Kon's destiny was to follow him.

Kon's presence must have intimidated the other birds and animals, for after he had departed they began to come more boldly into the clearing. Crows alighted on the ground beside her, cawing loudly and pecking at scraps of food left behind, peering at her with their fearless eyes, as if they hoped the flesh that covered her bones would soon become carrion.

Some animal, either a small wolf or a very large fox, lurked every evening on the edge of the clearing. She heard it hunting in the night, heard the sudden short scream of its prey. She was wary of it, knowing that, when winter came, wolves would move southward through the Darkwood. She remembered hearing them howling on snowy nights when she was a child at Matsutani. Sometimes, made desperate by hunger, they would attack the horses. Being awakened by the screaming horses, the snarling wolves, and the shouts of men running to drive them away was one of her enduring memories. In the morning there would be dead wolves to skin—their furs made warm winter coverings or chaps for riding—and wounded horses to put down, with the promise of fresh meat for days to come.

But she was most cautious of the wild boar, which, as autumn drew into winter, she often heard crashing through the undergrowth. She had seen dogs and men ripped open by their tusks. They were aggressive, seemed half-mad, even when they were not being hunted. She did not dare venture far from the clearing in case she was attacked by one. Yet staying where she was made her anxious, too. Yoshi had ordered the acrobats to say nothing about her, but they could so easily let slip a casual word and betray her.

The acrobats had left her food, and wood for the fire, which she kept going diligently. There was a grove of chestnut trees near the spring and the nuts were ripening. She collected them, storing them like a squirrel. But every night was a little colder than the last. Soon it would begin to freeze and then it would snow. *I will have to spend the winter in the hot spring if Take does not return*, she thought, but the reality, she knew, was she could not survive there.

Sometimes her passive waiting infuriated her. She longed to act. For so many years she had been told what to do by Fuji, had submitted to everything asked of her and suppressed all her own hopes and desires. Now she was free of all constraints, except those imposed by the weather and the changing seasons, and the frailty of her own body. Yet she did not know what action she could take.

In the short hours of daylight she took out the medicine stone and the Kudzu Vine Treasure Store. The Abbess had been right. In some way that Hina did not fully understand, the stone made the text readable. If she kept her left hand on the stone, she found she could not only read but understand what she read. As a child she had longed to make people and animals well, riven by pity for their suffering. Now that childish pity had turned into a mature, all-encompassing compassion.

So she made a virtue out of her solitude, overcoming her fears and her hunger, until she had completely absorbed the teachings of the text. She had grown so used to being alone that when a man and a tall brown horse appeared in the clearing one morning, for a moment she could not recognize what they were. They seemed one strange being, threatening and unpredictable. So they had come for her. She wanted to hide, but there was no time.

The man dismounted, calling her name. It was Chika, whom she had last seen when he came to Fuji's boat—or had she seen his shape underwater, the night Fuji died? He had come then to ask her to help Shikanoko. Her heart began to beat faster with excitement. Was it, at last, the time for Chika to take her to him?

He slid down from the horse's back and came to her, dropped to one knee, and bowed his head. The horse pulled on the reins, trying to reach the grass.

"Hina! I was told I would find you here."

Excitement and hope made her greet him warmly, despite his familiar tone. "I am so glad to see you, Chika," she said eagerly. "What news do you bring?"

He stood again, not speaking for a moment, studying her face with an intense expression that made her uncomfortable. She took a step back as she said, "I have no food to offer you, but let me take your horse to the spring to drink and I will bring back fresh water."

"I don't need anything," he said, dropping the reins. "The horse can find water if it's thirsty. Let's sit down and talk."

The sun was just beginning to clear the trees. Hina led

him to a patch of sunlight on the western side of the spring. The horse went to drink deeply, snorting through its nose. The ground was still cold. Hina sat on a small outcrop of rock. Chika pulled his sword from his sash and laid it down, then squatted on his haunches next to her.

"I've come from Kitakami," he said. "The brothers I told you about, Master Kikuta and Mu, have been reconciled, making the Tribe, as they call themselves, stronger than ever."

"And Shikanoko?" Hina said, his name filling her with joy and nervousness.

"Mu has gone to find him," Chika said.

"Will he bring him here?"

He frowned as though her eagerness distressed him and did not answer her question. "I've been thinking while I've been riding. I've had a lot of time lately to reflect on my life. I am not proud of what I have become."

"None of us can avoid our fate," Hina said.

"Maybe that is true, or maybe what proves a man is striving against fate and having the will to mold it to his own design. I am a warrior's son, Hina. It's a long time since I've lived as a warrior."

He put out a hand impulsively and gripped her thigh, his touch sending shock waves through her. "Aritomo is planning an attack on the Kakizuki in Rakuhara, to be led by your old patron, Arinori. That's why Arinori gave up his pursuit of you. Masachika knows you came into the Darkwood with the acrobats, he will find out where you are and will certainly come after you sooner or later. But Kiku, who has informants everywhere now, even in the capital, has already sent messengers to Lord Keita. The Kakizuki will be prepared and the Miboshi will be defeated. It's a chance for us to flee together. We can ride south and find the Kakizuki. We are of the same class, our families have been linked for generations. Ever since we were children I dreamed we would marry one day—I told you this before."

"But what about Shikanoko?" Hina said.

"You asked if Mu would bring him here. He will but he will be leading him to his death. Kiku says he wants to be of service to Shika, to restore the Emperor, but what he really wants is the mask Shika wears. I told you my sister's dream. I believe it means that you could remove the mask. But if Kiku takes possession of it, you will have condemned Shikanoko to death. He has said as much to me. In fact, he ordered me to kill him. Come with me and you will save not only your life but his, too."

His touch was embarrassing her with its intimacy and she tried to move from under it.

He looked at his own hand as if in surprise and lifted it away. "I'm sorry. I should not touch you. But you have had so many men and I have wanted you for so long. Won't you look with favor on me? I will take you away to safety. You can't stay here on your own. Masachika's men will find you eventually, if you aren't killed by wild animals first."

When she did not reply he went on. "We killed Unagi, you know, his sons and his father. I did it partly for you, so you would never be insulted by him again. And Kiku wanted to get rid of him. But once it was done I felt that part of my life was over. Or maybe Mu coming changed every-thing. I thought I was as close to Kiku as anyone, but Mu has become closer. I realized I was weary to death of that world of sorcerers and imps. I will never belong in it. Can you understand my loneliness? Kiku has offered me women, but I will never be able to meet and marry anyone of my own rank and I will not accept anyone else. But if we go to the Kakizuki, you, Kiyoyori's daughter, shall be the wife of Kongyo's son."

"That is impossible," she said, staring at him, shocked by his words. "I pity you deeply, but I was very fond of Unagi and, as I said to you before, he was a good man. I can't marry the man who killed him."

"I could show you I am a better man and a better lover. What's more, I am offering you a chance to escape, to save your life. You have no choice, Hina." He grasped both her arms as if he would lift her up. "You must come with me. I'll carry you if I have to!"

There was a crashing and rustling in the undergrowth and the horse squealed in fear. It threw up its head and barged past Chika, unbalancing him and knocking him to the ground. Suddenly released, Hina fell on her hands and knees.

She looked at the undergrowth, the sun dazzling her. The crashing noise came again and a huge boar, the largest she had ever seen, came bursting out, head down, charging toward them.

Its long tusks gleamed, its little eyes were red with rage, streams of saliva dripped from its glistening mottled snout. Each bristle stood out as sharp as a needle.

Chika lunged at her, not looking back at the boar.

"Chika!" She tried to shout out a warning.

He saw her gaze and turned, struggling to his feet, stumbling, reaching vainly for his sword.

The boar hit him like a galloping horse, thrust its tusks into him, and ripped him open with a sideways flick of its head.

It tossed him aside. There was a moment of silence and then he began to sob in pain.

"Hina!" he cried. "Help me!"

But she did not need the medicine stone to see he was dying.

The boar pawed the ground, peered at her with its vicious eyes. She walked slowly backward, staring fixedly at it through her tears, not daring to lift a hand to wipe them from her eyes, trying to calm her breath.

She saw its muscles tense as it prepared to charge. It seemed to gather itself up in a solid ball of aggression and rage. There was a humming sound through the air, like a giant insect, the thud of an impact, arrow into flesh. The boar squealed and hesitated for a moment, then launched itself at her, further enraged by pain. Another thrumming, a second arrow. The animal squealed again, a piercing, almost human sound, faltered, and dropped at her feet. Within seconds the light had gone from its eyes.

One shaft had hit it in the throat, the other protruded from its back, its white feathers now flecked red with blood. The arrowhead had penetrated straight to the heart.

12

MASACHIKA

Lord Aritomo traveled to Matsutani by palanquin, his favorite horse led behind by grooms, his bow and his sword carried by high-ranking warriors. Two falconers followed with his hawks on wooden perches. A monk from Ryusonji carried a bamboo cage containing the two young werehawks, which squawked and flapped their wings incessantly. The priests had managed to capture them and had presented them to Aritomo. The lord spoke to them every day and tended them with his own hands. The hawks disliked them intensely.

Aritomo's companions were all heavily armed and more than usually vigilant. Casting his eye over the procession as they rode out, Masachika, who had gone back to Miyako to escort his lord to his home, noticed that many warriors were absent, not from the highest caste, but from the ambitious middle ranks, and particularly those from the coastal estates who had some knowledge of boats and the sea. So the planned attack on the Kakizuki was going ahead, and, while Aritomo was entertained by the hunt, his old enemies would be taken by surprise and wiped out.

Yet there was little sense of celebration. Drought and famine had ravaged the land. The dead lay unburied along the roadsides and on the banks of the shrunken rivers. Crows stalked among them, the only creatures to look plump and sleek. Survivors threw stones at the birds; Masachika knew only too well how easily their aim could be turned on him and Aritomo's retinue.

Sometimes women knelt in the road, holding out starving children, begging the men for food, or, if they would give them nothing, pleading with them to put an end to their wretched lives and their children's suffering. The grooms chased them away with whips.

The mood among the warriors was somber. Death was everywhere, ignoble, insignificant, and inevitable. The wasted corpses, carrion for birds, mocked their own strength and vitality.

Look at us. You, too, will be reduced to bones like us. You, too, are no more than meat that will rot and putrefy.

At night, in the private homes or temples used as lodging places, Aritomo could not sleep, and those closest to him were summoned to sit up with him and listen to his thoughts on the way to live and the way to die.

"A warrior must choose his own death. Even on the battlefield, if he is defeated, it is better to die by his own hand than surrender to an opponent."

Death for him was another enemy, like drought and famine. He would defeat all three of them. A smile played on his lips as he regarded his men, as though he knew a secret they did not. He brewed and drank the strange-smelling tea all night, but never offered it to anyone else. Watching him closely, as he did all the time, Masachika could not help thinking how easy it would be to poison him. The more he tried to put the thought from him, the more he found himself dwelling on it.

Sometimes Aritomo spoke of Takaakira, with grudging respect. "As I grow older I admire courage above all virtues. In the end it is the only one that matters. To live without fear of death is to be a true warrior."

Masachika knew the hunt in the Darkwood would offer many opportunities to display fighting skills. The men would compete with one another to bring down the fiercest boar, the proudest stag. They might even be lucky enough to encounter bears. There were still vast tracts of land in the west and northeast that needed to be occupied and subdued. Warriors who acquitted themselves well in the hunt would be rewarded by Lord Aritomo with gifts of these lands. It was the next best thing to distinguishing oneself in battle, and for men eager to establish themselves and their families on estates granted to them forever, it offered a better chance of survival. Yet even hunting could be dangerous.

Shortly after they headed north from the barrier on the Shimaura road, at the turn to Matsutani, Masachika, riding ahead, heard singing, the sounds of a flute, and the chattering of monkeys. He saw the red of the acrobats' clothes. He urged his horse forward and ordered the entertainers to conceal themselves, for he wanted their appearance to be a complete surprise.

Obediently they pulled the pack horses over the dike, down into the dry rice fields. There were several men and, as far as he could see, eight monkeys. There was also a group of six musicians, carrying their instruments. The flute player had been playing, as they walked, and two of the women had been singing. The way the women moved and sang, freely, easily, reminded him of Asagao, with the now familiar but still astonishing surge of desire.

"Get down!" he told them, and they all prostrated themselves. Masachika watched from the top of the dike as Aritomo's retinue rode past. He did not want any of his entertainers shot by overzealous warriors. He could hear the werehawks shrieking even more loudly than usual and wondered what had alarmed them. When they had all passed by, he called to one of the older men to approach him.

"Come to Matsutani tomorrow, in the afternoon. We will be out at the hunt. We will expect your entertainment when we return. A little music first, I think, then acrobats with monkeys, and music for the rest of the evening. It must be a surprise, so do not show yourselves before then."

"I understand, lord," the man replied. "We will find a quiet spot to prepare ourselves and do our final rehearsals. We are all here now. Thank you for your confidence in us. We won't let you down."

"You had better not," Masachika replied.

Out of the corner of his eye he saw a huge black bird

fluttering down to the dike. He had come to hate with all his heart the crows that fed on carrion along the road, and was inclined to string his bow and shoot it. But it was not a crow. *One of the werehawks has escaped*, he thought, and was on the point of calling to the monk, but then he saw this bird was larger and not all black but flecked with gold patches that flashed blindingly in the sun. It unsettled him. He felt it must have some significance, but he could not unravel it, and he must not let Lord Aritomo travel on without him.

He caught up with the procession, dismounted, and walked beside the palanquin.

"Not long now, lord," he murmured. "We are nearly there."

The west gate stood open. Tama waited inside, with her women and retainers. Masachika contemplated their appearance with pleasure and pride—the women's layered robes in autumn hues, the men's new brilliant green hunting robes. Scarlet maples framed the view of the mountains in the east, and mandarins on a small tree by the steps glowed orange. The gardens and the house were immaculate, not a single stray leaf or unwelcome insect to be seen. The weather was perfect, neither clouds nor breeze, just the blue sky fading into pink and violet as the sun set and the first stars appeared. He felt a surge of satisfaction and, of course, gratitude to Tama, but he could not help searching for Asagao among the women.

They all bowed to the ground and murmured expressions

of welcome, as Aritomo was helped from the palanquin. He stumbled a little but then regained his balance, acknowledging the greetings with a slight nod. Masachika had left his horse at the gate, and had not failed to bow to Sesshin's eyes and the gateposts. Now he came forward, not offering an arm to help his lord lest that should offend him, but alert to any sign of weakness or dizziness.

"Masachika," Aritomo said, turning back. "That is the gate with the famous eyes, is it not?"

"It is, lord."

"Ah," Aritomo sighed. "To think I have talked with their owner. You would not guess what I have learned from him."

He looked at Masachika with his own unfathomable eyes. Masachika tried to make his expression opaque, fearing Aritomo could see all his desires and ambitions.

"I thought I heard voices as I passed under the gate." Aritomo was deeply interested in supernatural phenomena. "Do the eyes have the power of speech as well?"

"There are guardian spirits within the gateposts," Masachika said. "They are entirely benevolent."

"They sounded agitated," Aritomo said, and stepped onto the veranda. A stool had been prepared for him and maids came forward to wash the dust from his feet. He did not say more but gave Masachika another searching look. The caged werehawks were squabbling and shrieking.

Masachika bowed again, and as he rose, was approached by one of Tama's women who whispered that her mistress had gone farther into the garden, and this would be a good time for them to talk. She emphasized her words in a meaningful way that irritated him. All he wanted now was to be with Asagao. She was not with the women on the veranda, but he thought he could hear snatches of music from the pavilion where she was staying. Sighing heavily, he went to the lakeside where Tama was pacing to and fro.

"Don't walk around in that unattractive manner," he said. "You look less than calm."

"Calm?" she retorted. "I hardly know the meaning of the word anymore."

"What's the matter? Everything's going fine. The house, the garden, look magnificent. Come with me to Lord Aritomo, so he can congratulate you as I am sure he—"

She did not wait for him to finish. "The spirits are very upset. I've been doing all I can to placate them."

"That's the last thing we need! What have you done that's annoyed them?"

"I? I have done nothing. It is you who has outraged them. Ever since you came here with that girl . . ."

"Don't start on that again," Masachika said, affecting a weary tone. "I've told you, she means nothing to me."

"Then send her away." Tama stared at him defiantly.

"I won't do that. I need her for the entertainment I have arranged. The rest of the troupe will arrive tomorrow. We passed them on the road. I made them hide behind the bank; it was very amusing! We will hold the first hunt, and the entertainers will be ready in the evening, when we return. Do we have enough torches, and enough to drink?"

"Everything is prepared, Masachika. You don't need to supervise me, and don't try to change the subject. You, of all people, should know that the spirits should not be treated lightly. We made a vow before them, and I have had to make others to convince them that you are not lying. I have staked my life on your sincerity. I promised, if you proved untrue, I would kill myself. Look, you know the dagger I always carry with me?" She brought it out from her sash. "I am ready to use it at any time."

"Don't try to bully me, Tama. I will not be dictated to, by you or anyone. There is no need for such dramatic behavior. I have told you, the girl means nothing to me, but even if she did, what of it? Men take mistresses and concubines— why shouldn't I? It is expected in my position. You should consider yourself fortunate I don't have a whole string of them." He added spitefully, "If I did, one of them might give me a son."

"If you came to me more often, I would give you children," she said in a low voice. "And a string of women would be preferable to one who has won your heart."

"You are completely unreasonable," he said. "And don't start weeping. Your tears repulse me and you must not appear before our visitors with red eyes. Go inside and take control of yourself. And then get on with the many things that need to be done. It is almost dark. We must prepare for the feast."

"I have given you everything, Masachika, and I will take it all away from you." She looked at the dagger in her hand, with an almost tender smile. "Just one word in Aritomo's ear . . ."

"There is a special place in Hell reserved for women

who betray their husbands," he replied. He did not feel in the least threatened by her. If anything, her outburst proved the strength of her love for him. But he was not going to reveal to Aritomo's men how much she had always dominated him, nor was he going to yield to her. He did not believe for a moment that she would kill herself, or that she would divulge his secret conversation with the Emperor's mother. As for the spirits, he would deal with them in the morning, reprimand them and make sure they knew whom they had to obey.

He watched Tama walk away and, when she had disappeared into the house, went to the pavilion and ran across the stepping-stones, calling Asagao's name.

A wide plain lay to the southwest of Matsutani, between the forested mountains and the rice fields. It had no water, so was useless for cultivation, but it was a fine place for both hunting and hawking. Tama had arranged for more than fifty farmers to come from the surrounding villages to act as beaters for the hunt. From dawn the next day their shouts, drumming, and the clash of cymbals echoed through the Darkwood, as they drove animals into the range of the hunters. It was dangerous work—the men were armed only with staves, one broke a leg falling from a high cliff, two were gored by wild boars that came hurtling out of the bushes— but also enjoyable. They would be rewarded with some of the meat and it was a break from the daily toil of wresting a living from the land. The tasks of autumn awaited. The rice had been harvested and women were threshing and winnowing the husks, and shelling beans into huge baskets. Manure had to be spread on the fields, the woods close to the village coppiced for flexible branches that would be used in building and basket making, rice straw dried to make sandals, reeds cut for thatching, firewood gathered for the long weeks of snow. Beating for the hunt was a holiday.

The warriors wore chaps of fur or deerskin and hunting robes stained with persimmon sap, or in colors of green and cream, printed with autumn flowers and grasses. The horses' reins were dyed blue or purple, the saddles decorated with silver lacquer, the girths braided with gold thread.

As they galloped over the plain, bringing down the panicked animals, Aritomo watched from the back of his dapple gray horse. He wore bearskin chaps and a hat of silk, with a motif of pines, a compliment to Masachika, to whom he had entrusted his sword and his bow. His falconers sat on horses behind him, each with a hawk on his wrist.

A little farther back stood a huge man, holding the white banner of the Miboshi.

Masachika thought the lord looked better than he had for several weeks. The fresh air, the new surroundings, the excitement of the hunt had made the blood flow more strongly through his veins. His spirits seemed high, too; he was in a generous mood and the successful hunters were rewarded with gifts of land of hundreds of acres.

Masachika wore a hunting robe of light willow green, patterned with flocks of plovers. His chaps were gray wolf skins and his hunting arrows were fletched with tawny and white hawk feathers. His bow was bound with wisteria vine and he rode his favorite tall black horse, Sumi. His sedge hat was lined with pale blue silk.

Sumi was restless, pawing the ground and shaking his head frequently. His skin twitched with every shout and every clash of the cymbals. Masachika was cramped and uncomfortable. He turned his irritation onto Lord Aritomo, who sat without moving, and allowed it to fester into bitter anger. As the host, he was obliged to leave the best opportunities to his guests, but it riled him to see so many of them distinguish themselves and be rewarded, while he had to content himself with holding Lord Aritomo's weapons.

He had to watch while one man killed a boar, bringing it down right in front of Lord Aritomo; another returned in the late afternoon, a huge black bear, with thick fur and gleaming teeth, slung over his horse's back. He presented it to Lord Aritomo and it was graciously accepted, and a large estate at the foot of the High Cloud Mountains granted in payment. Masachika added words of congratulations that nearly choked him.

When the sun began to descend toward the west, Aritomo indicated he would like to return. A conch shell was blown to signify the end of the hunt and his warriors began to gather around him for the ride back. The men's faces were flushed with excitement; the horses breathed heavily, their flanks heaving, white with sweat.

Masachika gave Aritomo's weapons to one of the bodyguards and let the men go on ahead, while he arranged for the slaughtered animals to be collected and carried home, where they would be skinned, some of the meat distributed to the beaters, the rest prepared for the evening's feast. As well as deer and boar, and the bear, there were serow, wolves and foxes, rabbits and hares, squirrels, pheasants, marmots, raccoons. Tusks and antlers would be removed, the larger ones saved for helmet decorations, the smaller used for knife handles and other carvings.

The number of dead deer astonished him—could there be any left alive in the Darkwood? He rode through the temporary dwellings erected for the warriors, greeting many and accepting their thanks and compliments. A wooden platform had been constructed, facing the lake, where Aritomo would eat and watch the performers. The lake had shrunk so much in the years of drought, there was a wide expanse of sand on the shoreline. At one end, food was being prepared in an outdoor kitchen, at the other was the small stage for the musicians. The acrobats would perform on the sand. They had requested a boat, as well, and a small one lay at the water's edge.

Already, from behind the silk curtain that defined the end of the stage, Masachika could hear the chattering of monkeys, and a plangent twanging as the musicians tuned their instruments. He dismounted, told the groom who had been walking beside him to take the horse to the stable, and went behind the curtain.

The music stopped and everyone immediately bowed to him. There were two young men, about twenty years old, he thought, four somewhat older, and two who looked well into their thirties, already showing signs of age. Several of them had monkeys already sitting on each shoulder, tethered with braided blue silk cords, fastened to leather collars set with mother-of-pearl and blue gemstones. The monkeys had thick gray and white fur, their faces and rumps were rose pink, and their deep-set eyes, hazel or green. They wore the same sleeveless red jackets as the acrobats.

The music group consisted of the flute player he had heard on the road, a drummer, the two women singers, and a lutist. There was no sign of Asagao.

He asked where she was and one of the singers replied, "She has gone to get the other lute; her own has a broken string."

He was tempted to follow her, and lie with her quickly, before the night's celebrations started. The idea excited him unbearably. He checked that everything was ready and went to enter the garden by the east gate, from where it would be easy to slip unnoticed into the pavilion. But his wife was standing on the veranda, directing a flurry of maids and servants who were carrying bowls, cushions, eating trays, and so on to the lakeshore.

She saw him and, giving some last instruction to the steward, stepped down from the veranda and came toward him. Her face was pale, her eyes, despite his admonitions, red rimmed.

"What's the matter?" he said sharply.

Her voice was expressionless and cold. "Have you been to the west gate?"

"No, I came in the other way."

"Come with me now."

"I am busy now," Masachika said. "Besides, it is better not to disturb the spirits."

"You won't disturb them," Tama said. "They are not there."

She walked swiftly to the gate and stood between the posts. The evening's offerings lay scattered about as though someone had kicked them away.

"I felt them go," she said. "They threw the offerings at my head and rushed past me."

"You are imagining it," Masachika said. "It is your own lack of composure that you are feeling. They have just decided to go quiet again."

"I don't think so. They have escaped. They released the two werehawks Lord Aritomo brought with him." She looked up. "The birds were flying around shrieking, but I can't hear them now. Well, it doesn't matter. You have lied to me and to the spirits, and now my life is forfeit. I only hope that will be enough to placate them, and that they will not ruin the estate after my death."

"Don't talk nonsense," he said, but more gently, for he was suddenly afraid she was losing her mind. "You are not going to kill yourself."

She did not reply, but gave him a look such as he had never seen before from her. Her contempt stabbed some inner part of him and he felt unexpected despair over all he was going to lose.

"Tama, I beg you. Don't do it. The girl means nothing to me. I will send her away tomorrow."

"It is too late," she replied.

He took refuge in anger, then, as was his habit. "How can

you bother me with your fantasies at a time like this? I have so many things to think about. We will talk tonight—I will come to you, it will be between us as it used to be, I promise you. Now, let us present a night's entertainment that Lord Aritomo will never forget."

"And your plan to hasten his end?" she said scornfully.

"Don't speak of such things!" He looked anxiously around the garden, as though they might be overheard.

"If you do have the courage to do it, you will have to write your own poems to the Emperor," she said, and walked away from him.

Masachika heard a bird call and, looking up, saw, perched on the roof, the strange black bird he had noticed in the rice fields. He could just make out its outline against the darkening sky. The streaks of gold glimmered in the last of the light. He waved his arms at it, but it did not move.

"I will deal with you in the morning," he vowed.

From the house to the lakeshore, the garden blazed with light. Oil lamps, candles, torches, the kitchen fires at the northern end on which the beasts were roasting, all competed with the huge orange moon that was rising behind the mountains.

Persimmon moon, Masachika thought, with an uneasy feeling of premonition. It was the last thing he wanted Aritomo to see. Fortunately, by the time Aritomo had finished eating, the moon had changed its color and was high enough to throw a silver path across the lake's surface.

Aritomo commented on it as he took another cup of wine. "Even the moon conspires to make us feel at home. Masachika, you and your wife have excelled yourselves. I cannot remember a more delightful day."

"It is nothing," Masachika replied. "However, still to come is a humble little entertainment I have arranged for your pleasure."

Aritomo gave one of his rare smiles and leaned forward in anticipation.

A wide mat was unrolled on the shore and the silk curtain of the stage drawn to one side. Behind it, the musicians were seated, with a few lamps lighting their faces. Masachika could see Asagao quite clearly, her delicate features, the curve of her breast. She held the shabby old lute, which seemed a shame, but it was the only displeasing aspect. He could not believe he was being forced to give up this beautiful girl. He felt a surge of anger against his wife. He suppressed the fear he had felt earlier and took comfort in memories of how Tama had come to him in Minatogura, her pleas, her expressions of love, repeated so many times in so many nights over the years. In the end she always yielded to him. This time would be no different.

There was a sudden clacking of sticks, announcing the beginning of the performance, and the loud pounding of a drum. As the other musicians joined in, Masachika could hear the lute. It was slightly out of tune and its notes sounded reluctant. Asagao was frowning and she glanced at the other lute player, who made a swiftly hidden grimace in response.

Aritomo, who had a fine ear for music, was also frowning.

"Well, it is, after all, country-style music," he said graciously. "We cannot expect the skills of the court here."

Masachika bowed his head in response, trying to stay calm, wondering why Asagao was playing so badly. Had Tama, or the guardian spirits, cast a spell on her?

The small boat floated into the moonlight path, lit by two torches blazing in its stern. Three monkeys were perched in it, wearing courtiers' robes, with black silk hats on their heads. One held a fan, one a wine flask, and the third beat a rhythm on a small drum.

The boat nudged against the shore and the monkeys stepped out gracefully. They walked on their hind legs toward Aritomo and bowed to the ground in his direction. Then they turned to the south and bowed to the guests, and to the north, to the musicians.

Three acrobats came out of the darkness, tumbling across the mat in a series of cartwheels and somersaults. They seized a monkey each and threw them into the air. The monkeys landed nimbly on the men's shoulders and then leaped sideways from shoulder to shoulder, as if they were being juggled.

Something in the music changed, as if the lute had stopped resisting the player. Masachika heard Aritomo gasp in surprise. He followed his gaze to Asagao. Somehow, when they weren't looking, she had changed lutes. She was now holding one of rare beauty, its cherrywood frame and mother-of-pearl inlay gleaming in the torchlight. And music poured from it, almost celestial in its purity and perfection, leaving even Asagao open-mouthed with amazement.

The bird, perched somewhere unseen, sang in harmony with it.

For a few moments the audience watched and listened, transfixed, not sure if it was some magic trick or if they were witnessing a miracle.

Aritomo looked from the lute to the acrobats and back again. Then he was on his feet, his face white, his eyes blazing.

"Arrest them," he said, trying to speak forcefully, but failing. His voice was a croak. "Seize them immediately."

"Lord?" Masachika said, bewildered.

"That is Genzo—the imperial lute that has been lost since the rebellion. One of those young men is Yoshimori!"

13

TAMA

Once she had seen that the food was prepared and everything was running smoothly, Tama slipped away to her room. She performed all her tasks with a detached tenderness, knowing each one was for the last time. Haru alone noticed her leave, and rose to follow her, but Tama made a sign to her to stay where she was. Haru would try to dissuade her, and she was determined not to be turned away from her purpose.

The house was empty. All of them, servants, maids, guards, were on the lakeshore, attending to guests, hoping to see the performers. A few lamps had been lit, and their flames burned steadily in the still air. She glanced almost indifferently at the cypress floors, each perfect plank selected by her, at the silk wall hangings and all the valuable carvings and vases that she had chosen and had displayed discreetly throughout the house. She marveled that all she had once loved so much now meant nothing to her.

The main rooms of the house faced south and east. The room in which she lived was on the northwest side. The moonlight did not penetrate it, but the shutters had not been closed and the shadows the moon threw hovered in the garden. Moths were fluttering around the lamp flame and she could hear the thin whining of mosquitoes. From the garden came the melancholy chirping of insects that had only days to live.

But even that is longer than I have.

She went to her writing desk and found her inkstone and brush. There was still enough water in the dropper to wet the stone. She took out a few sheets of paper, enfolded in a silk cloth, and unwrapped them, shaking out the fragments of rue and aloewood that had been placed among them. Everything was attacked by insects, nothing was exempt from the universal rule of death. The only courageous act was to snatch control from death itself, to decide the time and manner of one's own departure. The thought made her smile.

I will compose a poem on that, but first I will write my testament so that no one misunderstands my reasons.

Matsutani no Tama, daughter of Tadahise, wife of Kiyo-yori and Masachika . . .

She felt a slight movement in the air beside her.

"What is the Matsutani lady doing?"

"Is she getting ready to kill herself?"

"She has to, she made us a vow."

"So why doesn't she get on with it?"

Tama said, "I am writing a few things down first." She

was glad they were there with her. "Then, I promise you, I will not hesitate."

"We can trust the Matsutani lady."

"Not like the Matsutani lord, so-called."

"He's a liar."

"Yes, he tells lies."

"I know he does," Tama said. "I know all his faults. I loved him despite them. Maybe I still love him . . . now, please be quiet so I can think clearly."

There were a few moments of silence, then one of them— she still could not tell them apart, but she thought it might be Hidarisama, as he usually spoke first—said in a sulky voice: "I feel like throwing things."

"Oh, so do I!"

"Let's go throw things at the Matsutani lord."

"So-called."

"No," Tama said firmly. "The throwing must not start again. Not until after I am dead. Then you can do what you like."

She wrote swiftly, putting down her reasons for dying, on this night, by her own hand. Not only Matsutani's unfaithfulness to her, but his willingness to betray Lord Aritomo and the secrets he had kept from him; the intrigue with Lady Natsue; Kiyoyori's daughter, Hina; Akihime's son.

There, that should condemn him, she thought with mingled satisfaction and sorrow. A whisper came from beside her.

"How will she do it?"

"With her knife. She is taking it out now."

"Oh, good, I want to see blood."

"Oh, so do I!"

Tama felt the blade with her thumb. A thin strip of blood sprang out of her skin. She let a few drops fall on a new sheet of paper on which she wrote.

At the Shirakawa barrier,
The one I desired awaited me.
I called him back.
We lay together in the cattail grasses.
He gave me life's dew. I gave him death's.

"Make sure Lord Aritomo reads these," she said, laying aside the brush and taking up the dagger. Without hesitation she put it to her throat and, leaning forward so her own weight helped her hand, cut fiercely from left to right. She felt the sudden shock in her nerves, her body's realization that a catastrophe had taken place. Her blood felt warm on her hands.

As she fell forward she heard music, so beautiful it dealt her a further shock.

It is the Enlightened One coming for me.

Then she just had time to realize it was a lute, playing by the lakeside. Could it be Asagao who was so talented? Tears of envy and regret came to her eyes, and she wept for her own passing from this world.

14

MASACHIKA

Masachika could not believe his good fortune. The promised surprise was far greater than he could have imagined. Within moments the acrobats were surrounded. The monkeys leaped away, screaming in shock and fear. The musicians were seized, their instruments taken from them and thrown into a pile, except for the lute, which was carried reverently to Lord Aritomo.

It still played exuberantly as though there was nothing to fear, nothing to regret.

Aritomo looked at it without speaking. A murmur began to run through the watching crowd. *It is the Emperor! It is the Emperor!* One by one the servants fell to their knees.

As Aritomo reached out to touch the lute, warriors ran to get their weapons. Aritomo turned his gaze on the acrobats.

"Bring the two young ones to me," he commanded, and

when they had been forced to their knees before him said, "One of you is the son of the rebel Momozono. Which is it?"

They exchanged a swift look in which Masachika thought he saw recognition, acceptance.

"I am!" the shorter one said defiantly.

Masachika knew he was lying. It was obvious to him which was Yoshimori; he was surprised he had not recognized him before. Without knowing it he had brought Yoshimori to Aritomo, and Asagao and her lute had revealed him. *Tama will forgive me everything now!*

"It is the taller one, lord," he said.

"Yes, I think so, too. Well, we will execute them both. Prepare the ground. You may carry out the act yourself. I cannot praise you highly enough, Masachika. You have done what no one else could do. First the Autumn Princess, now the false pretender. Name your reward. I will give you half the realm."

"I desire nothing but to serve you," Masachika replied. "I will fetch my sword."

As he went toward the house he thought he heard Asagao calling his name, but he ignored her. He would have to let her go now; he would not be able to save her. He wanted above all to find Tama and tell her the news.

At the threshold Haru met him. He could not see her clearly, but something in her face, her posture brought him to a halt.

"Don't go inside," she said.

"What is wrong? I must fetch my sword and speak to my wife, but I must hurry. Lord Aritomo is waiting."

"Lady Tama is dead. There is a great deal of blood."

"I don't believe you! Let me see her!"

"You should not go inside. The guardian spirits are in there. They told me to take these papers to Lord Aritomo."

Masachika made a grab at them. "Give them to me! I command you as your lord!"

She evaded him. "I never served you, Masachika. My husband and I served Lord Kiyoyori."

He was taller than she was and much stronger. She was made confused and slow by shock. He was about to overpower her and take the papers from her when the two young werehawks swooped down, striking at him with their beaks and talons. He let go of the woman to protect his face and Haru ran into the garden toward the lakeshore.

Masachika hesitated for a moment but decided the most important thing was to get his sword. He stepped into the house, took it from the rack inside the entrance, and, drawing it, said, "I command you to return to the gateposts."

There was a long moment of silence and then one of the spirits said, "Who's that?"

"So-called Matsutani lord."

"The liar?"

"Yes, the liar and the traitor."

"We don't have to do what he says anymore!"

"No, never again!"

"And can we throw things now?"

"Yes! Yes!"

The first thing they threw was a lamp. It fell near Masachika, spilling oil on the matting. A little flicker of flame began to grow from it.

"Tama!" Masachika called. "Tama, come out!"

"The Matsutani lady is dead."

"She was brave."

"Not like the so-called Matsutani lord," they said together.

Their voices echoed after him as he ran from the house, sword in hand.

The crackle of burning followed him, the air became heavy with smoke.

The Matsutani lady is dead.

She had sworn to kill herself and she had kept her word, but why now? Why had she done it when his fortune was at its peak? They could have shared everything together. Asagao was already as dead to him. But could Tama really have betrayed him? He had to get the papers before Aritomo read them.

The moon was now directly overhead, its light shimmering on the still surface of the lake, on the swords of the warriors, showing clearly the two young men kneeling on the sand.

Their hands had been bound roughly behind them. The shorter one looked from side to side, obviously very afraid, but Yoshimori was quite calm, his face turned upward, his lips moving slightly as if he were praying. The monkeys had sought refuge with the older acrobats and were clinging to them, all except one who kept running to Yoshimori wailing like a human child. He shook his head at it, trying to gesture that it should go back to the others, and then resumed his silent prayer.

Asagao saw Masachika and called his name again. She

was in a huddle with the acrobats and musicians. Armed warriors had formed two circles, one around them, the other around Aritomo and the young men, keeping the crowd back. He saw Haru struggling to get through them, waving the papers, and he could hear her voice, shouting to Lord Aritomo to listen to her.

She had not yet reached Aritomo. Masachika felt a surge of relief and then a thud of excitement in his belly. He was going to execute the Emperor of the Eight Islands. He would never be overlooked again; his name would never be forgotten. He might not have killed a single animal in the hunt, but the greatest prize would be his.

He strode toward Aritomo. The warriors parted at his approach. He saw wonder and admiration in their eyes.

"I am ready, lord," he said, holding Jinan aloft.

Flames seemed to crackle along the blade, as a fireball shot into the air from the house. The three werehawks could be seen in its light, swirling above the roof.

"The house is on fire!" Aritomo cried. "What is happening? Is it the work of those guardian spirits I heard before?"

Masachika said, "I am here. Let us act immediately."

Aritomo did not reply to this but said, "Have the spirits escaped?"

"Don't worry about them! I can control them. We must not delay."

"But the house is burning. Where is your wife?"

Haru had forced her way after him and shrieked in reply, "She is dead, Lord Aritomo. She took her own life and she left this testament. You must read it at once!"

Aritomo heard her finally, and turned to her. Before Masachika could intercept he had taken the papers and entrusted them to one of his warriors. The heat was growing intense and sparks and ash were falling around them.

"We cannot stay here," Aritomo said. "If Lady Tama is indeed dead I will do her the honor of reading this later. But now I must make all haste to get away, for I believe this place is accursed. Masachika, you must stay, subdue the spirits, save your house if you can, and bury your wife. I will see you in Miyako."

"But the execution . . ." Masachika said, Jinan still in his hand, ready.

"It will take place in public in Miyako. That will put an end to the rumors and the unrest." Aritomo looked around at his elated warriors. "Secure the prisoners and prepare to leave immediately." Then he could not prevent himself from giving a great shout of triumph.

"I have Yoshimori and I will live forever!"

15

HINA

Hina stood motionless. She wondered if she would ever move again. The two arrows still quivered in the boar's flesh, one in its throat, one in its back.

Chika was lying next to it, crumpled, bloody, his sightless eyes staring up.

She heard a voice behind her ask, "Are you hurt?"

Could it be Take? So one of the arrows was his. Whose was the other?

Her heart, along with everything around her—the rustling leaves, the dappled sunlight, the chirruping birds—seemed to pause. She held her breath. Figures were moving out from the trees. The sunlight was behind them and she could make out only their shapes, as if they were shadows falling on a screen.

She saw the antlered outline of the man-deer.

Take said again, "Lady, are you hurt?"

"No." She could not take her eyes off the approaching group. She hardly registered the fact that Take had returned or questioned how he had got there. She heard him set another arrow to his bow.

"Don't shoot!" she cried.

"Do you know them?"

"It is Shikanoko, your father."

A strange-shaped wolflike animal walked on one side of him, and at his other shoulder an old silver white stallion.

"Nyorin," Hina whispered, and tears began to flow down her cheeks.

There were three men on horseback, two wearing black silk coverings across their faces, showing only their eyes. The third also had a scarf wound around his head, but it was a dark red color, madder-dyed. Behind him, his arms around his waist, was the fourth man. He made a half wave to them, and slid from the horse's back. He went swiftly to Chika and knelt beside him.

Hina did not think she knew him, but Take returned the greeting eagerly.

Pushing past the group came another white horse, black tail and mane, its head high, its eyes huge. It gave a shrill neigh and cantered up to Hina, stopping directly in front of her and lowering its head to breathe in her face.

"Tan?" she said wonderingly, put her arms around his neck, and laid her cheek against his smooth coat. She could feel his heartbeat.

When she stepped back, tears filled the horse's dark eyes and streaked his cheeks. She put out her hand to wipe them away, and then touched the salty wetness on her own cheeks.

"This is your twin," she said to Take. "You and he were born on the same day." Then she dared to look at Shikanoko, who was now standing within arm's reach. "I suppose Risu is dead?" she said. She could think of nothing else to say.

"She died years ago. We buried her in the mountains."

His voice had hardly changed. She would have known it anywhere. She had heard it in her dreams for years.

"Lady Hina," he said, speaking more formally, and dropped to one knee before her, bowing his antlered head.

"You do not have to bow to me," she cried. She put out one hand and touched the broken antler. She felt something spark beneath her fingers as if the air were full of lightning. She closed both hands around the polished bones, hardly noticing the flesh sear. Her tears fell for his humility, for the pain he had suffered and all he had endured. She lifted with both hands. For a moment it seemed she was trying to move an immense weight, rooted in the earth, and then, as her tears fell more freely, the heaviness dissolved and the mask floated, of its own accord, away from Shikanoko's face.

He cried out, from pain or surprise, she could not tell. She saw the gray-white color of the skin across his forehead, the tangled beard on his cheeks. His eyes blinked in the sudden intense light. His lips looked chapped and dry. He covered his face with his palms.

She knelt, still holding the mask, looking at its lacquered face as it became lifeless. It had been so easy, so quick, yet she knew something momentous had happened. "What shall I do with it?"

He took a bag, many layered, brocade, from his waist and held it open. It seemed too small to contain the mask, yet it slipped inside from her hands and he tied the cords.

She wanted to take his hands and look deep into his eyes, but he would not meet her gaze.

"I have worn the mask for over twelve years," he said. "I hardly remember what I was like before. I no longer know how to look at the world without it."

He seemed physically affected, almost on the verge of fainting. The two men in the black face coverings dismounted, gave their horses' reins to the red-scarfed one, and came to Shikanoko, kneeling beside him, embracing him. None of them spoke, as if they did not yet understand what the removal of the mask would mean.

Hina stood and stepped back, confused by so many emotions she could not speak. Was that all that was going to happen? Why had he not taken her in his arms? *I love him,* she thought, *but he does not love me.*

The man with the red scarf tethered the horses and began to uncover his head. Hina saw he was clean shaven, and grinning at her. When he spoke she realized it was a woman.

"Don't you recognize me, lady? And can this young man really be little Take? When I last saw you, you were a babe in arms. Lady Hina was jumping into the lake with you! You were both thought to be drowned."

"Bara?" Hina said, hardly believing it.

"No longer Bara, lady. I changed my name. Now it is Ibara. I have become as sharp and prickly as a thorn."

There were too many people, Hina thought, too many crosscurrents, from the past, from the future. She took a few more steps backward and found herself standing next to Take, who still had the arrow set to his bowstring and who had not ceased staring at Shikanoko.

She turned to look at him and saw he was wearing a blue jacket and bearskin chaps. His huge bow looked ancient, but his sword was newly fashioned. There was something outlandish about him, as though he had come from another world.

"How did you get here? Where have you been?"

"A tengu dropped me here," he replied lightly. "Just in time, too!"

"You saved my life," she said.

"I did not know whether to aim at the man or the boar," he said. "I did not know which was the greater danger to you."

"Poor Chika," she said, trembling as she recalled his hands on her.

"Who was he?"

"I knew him when I was a child." She did not want to say any more about him.

Tan rubbed his head gently on her shoulder. Nyorin also approached, whinnying at her. Standing between the two white stallions she felt their power, their steadfastness.

"Shikanoko!" she called.

He raised his head and looked at her. His eyes were

already accustomed to the light, but his face still wore a fragile, vulnerable look.

"Do this one thing for me and then I will never ask anything of you again."

He rose and came toward her. "What do you mean? My life is yours to command, however you wish."

"This is your son, Takeyoshi. I have looked after him since he was born. Now you must promise to take care of him." And then she added, in a low voice, "His mother was Akihime, the Autumn Princess."

Take dropped to his knees. "Sir . . . Father . . . I offer you my sword. It was forged for me by the tengu Tadashii, who was one of my teachers. The other was your companion, Master Mu."

Mu took the blade and examined it eagerly. "It's a good one," he exclaimed. "A brother to mine, which was also made by tengu."

"And this is the bow, Ameyumi, the Rain Bow, that we recovered," Take said, tentatively, standing and holding it out to Shikanoko.

He took it, gazing at it in wonder. "Ameyumi! I remember it from my childhood. It was lost when my father died in the north. And you can shoot, with a bow this size, and so accurately!"

"You must keep it," Take said.

Shikanoko handed the bow back to him. "No, it is fitting that it should be yours. I have its echo, Kodama." He reached out and touched Take's face. "To meet you after all these years is more than I could have ever imagined!

I hope we will never be parted." He looked around. "But where is Yoshimori?"

"He went with the acrobats," Hina replied. "They have gone to Matsutani to perform for Lord Aritomo, on the orders of Masachika, my uncle."

Tan pawed the ground and let out a shrill neigh.

"Why did he do that?" Take cried. "Why put himself in such danger?"

"He does not know who he is," Hina replied. "Or rather, he knows, but he chooses not to admit it. He is the Emperor, he goes where he wants to go."

"And we must follow him," Shikanoko said. "Ibara, let Chika's horse carry him. Takeyoshi can ride with me on Nyorin. And, Lady Hina, I believe Tan will be happy to carry you."

"No one else rides him, but Lady Hina can." Ibara was smiling, but then her expression changed as she went to Chika and began to arrange his clothes, binding his own sash around the terrible wound. Mu helped her and between them they slung the corpse across the tall brown horse, soothing it as it shuddered and rolled its eyes.

Shikanoko lifted Hina onto Tan's back. She felt her body longing to soften at the touch of his hands, but she tried to make her will fierce against him.

"You know who this horse is, don't you?" he said.

"Risu's foal. I saw him being born—on the same day as your son."

"But over and above that," Shikanoko said, gently, "the spirit within him is not a horse but that of your father, Lord Kiyoyori."

Tan's ears twitched and he whinnied as if he were laughing for joy.

"I called him back from where he walked on the banks of the river of death. Someone who owed him a great debt had taken his place on the ferry that plies between this world and the next. Your father was able to return to continue his struggle to restore the true emperor."

Hina leaned forward and clasped her arms around the horse's neck, laying her head on the thick, black mane. "Now I understand why I loved you so much," she whispered.

Often Take tired of riding and ran ahead. Hina wondered what the tengu's teaching had done for him to make him so tireless and so fast. Even when the horses cantered, as they frequently did, for their riders were all seized by the same sense of urgency, he could outstrip them. He had grown to his adult height and no longer had the slender limbs of a boy.

Shikanoko could not take his eyes off him, watched him almost hungrily, but he hardly looked at Hina, nor did he speak much to her though they often rode side by side.

As they approached Matsutani, and her eyes took in the scenes of her childhood from which she had been exiled for so many years, she became almost feverish. Her eyes glowed and her color was heightened.

Ibara said to Mu, "She was a beautiful child—I always imagined that was what saved her life—and now as a woman she is unparalleled. But maybe I am biased, having cared for her like my own child."

"She also has wisdom," Mu replied, "which gives her a rare inner beauty." He sighed. "Ah well, things will work out or they will not."

Ibara, who was sitting in front of him, jabbed him in the ribs with her elbow. "Sometimes we are called on to make them work out, my friend. Our lord may have been released from the mask, but his eyes have not yet been opened to what's in front of him."

Hina could hear what they were saying. The thought that Shikanoko probably could, too, made her color rise further.

"What will we find at Matsutani?" she wondered aloud. "Will Lord Aritomo still be there? Will Yoshimori be safe? And what about Haru, Chika's mother? Could she still be alive? What a terrible thing, to be bringing her son home, dead."

Shikanoko said, "We are very close now, no more than an hour or so away. I'll send the Burnt Twins ahead to see how things stand. Nagatomo was brought up at Kumayama, and is familiar with the whole area. Eisei has been to Matsutani and knows both Aritomo and Masachika by sight."

"Why are they called the Burnt Twins?" Hina asked, eager to keep him talking, but also genuinely curious about his loyal companions.

"They were both forced to wear the mask—it seared their skin. Out of their suffering came companionship and love. They are twinned souls."

"It burned my hands, too," she said, glancing at his face, which was slowly returning to a normal color. He had shaved away the beard. "Yet it did not burn you?"

"It was made for me. Only I can wear it, but in the encounter with the Prince Abbot some of his dying power condemned it to fuse to my face. I lived half man, half deer ever since, until you released me."

"It is so powerful," she said, remembering what Chika had told her.

"Powerful and dangerous," he replied, "So much that I fear using it. I hope I never have to place it on my face again." He stopped abruptly and after a few moments said, "You were able to do what no one else could, take it from me. But I am sorry about your hands."

"They are healing fast," she said, not quite truthfully, for they were still painful. It was lucky she could ride Tan without reins.

Now he will say something, she thought, but it seemed he felt he had already said too much. He turned in the saddle, beckoned to Nagatomo, and swiftly gave him instructions.

After Nagatomo and Eisei had left, the others dismounted to wait for their return. The horses grazed. Shikanoko went a little way off and sat in meditation, the wolflike creature at his side.

Hina went in the other direction, wondering if his thoughts were as distracted as hers. Take was helping Mu and Ibara make a small fire and prepare food. Then the three of them began to spar with poles they cut from saplings in the surrounding forest.

Hina was determined not to move before Shikanoko did. Slowly her mind stilled and she succeeded in dismissing all thoughts of him. Instead she concentrated on Yoshi, holding him up to Heaven, praying for his safety.

Time crawled past, as though the whole world had slowed and thickened. Around the end of the afternoon, when the shadows were lengthening and the air was growing colder, the wolflike creature got to its feet and walked stiffly to the path, gazing in the direction the Burnt Twins had taken.

"They are returning," Ibara said, lowering her pole, sidestepping Take's final lunge and laughing as it unbalanced him.

Eisei rode first, Nagatomo behind him, his horse slower because of its extra burden, a woman who clung to his waist.

Eisei called out, "Matsutani has burned to the ground. Aritomo has already left for the capital. The place was deserted except for this woman."

When Nagatomo dismounted and lifted her down, Hina saw it was Haru.

It was years since she had seen her, and Haru had turned into an old woman.

The birds had begun their evening chorus and, echoing through it, Hina heard a sharp call, echoed by another. Her heart seemed to stop and painfully start again. Was it Kon? If Kon had abandoned Yoshi, it could only mean he was dead.

Haru walked tentatively toward her, frowning as though she thought she knew her, eyes fixed on her.

Hina wanted to prevent her seeing her son's body and called to Ibara to move the horse, but her intention had the opposite effect, drawing Haru's gaze in that direction.

The woman gave a shriek, and stumbled toward the

corpse, which was hanging head down across the brown horse. She knelt in front of it, touching the cold swollen lips and the limp hands.

"What happened?" she said, turning to Hina. "Who was responsible?"

"He was killed by a boar," Hina said. "It was charging at me."

"He saved your life? At least he died well. What happened to the boar, did it live?"

"Shikanoko and his son killed it," Hina replied. She would not disabuse Haru of her belief, for Chika had been trying to save her life in his own way. Now his fate seemed unutterably sad. She wanted to weep for him and his mother.

"Shikanoko?" Haru looked around wildly. "Shikanoko is here? We thought he must be dead."

She saw him as he stood and moved toward them. "You have a son?" she cried. "Why is your son alive while mine is dead?"

She fell to the ground, sobbing, tearing at the earth with her hands.

"Haru," Shikanoko said, his voice both stern and gentle. "Chika is dead. We have brought his body back to bury wherever it pleases you. But there is no time for any excesses of grief. Where is the Emperor?"

At that moment two birds flew down with a clatter of wings and landed on Shikanoko's shoulder. Hina knew them at once as werehawks. For an instant, she noticed, Shikanoko flinched, but the birds were not attacking him. They bowed their heads and then whispered in his ear.

"Where did you come from?" he said. "Who brought you to Matsutani?"

They replied excitedly in their grating voices. Shikanoko said, "Yoshimori has been taken to Miyako. Kon has followed him. We must go after them."

The birds squawked in approval and then muttered something else.

"I suppose you are right," Shikanoko replied, and then addressed the others. "I must deal with the guardian spirits at Matsutani. We will go there first."

16

MASACHIKA

I should take my own life before I am shamed publicly. No, I gave Yoshimori to Aritomo, he will forgive me anything. Tama is dead. If only I knew what she wrote, to what extent she betrayed me. Maybe he will not read the papers at all. Why should he believe an old woman like Haru? I will follow him to Miyako. I will carry out the execution. Once Yoshimori is dead Daigen will be Emperor and his mother already favors me. Tama is dead.

All these thoughts raced through Masachika's mind as he watched Aritomo and his warriors leave and the house burn to the ground. Some of the servants made futile efforts to fetch water from the lake to douse the flames, but the spirits threw fireballs at them, followed by volleys of burning utensils and furniture. Eventually everyone gave up and ran away.

He spent the night in the pavilion where he had lain with Asagao such a short time ago. When day broke he saw the house was completely destroyed. Whatever had remained of Tama was reduced to ashes. Why had he treated her so badly? Why had he lied to her? He had satisfied his own desire even though it had wounded and humiliated her. They had had everything and he had smashed it. She and Matsutani had been given to him once, then ripped away by his father's cruel decision, then restored to him. She had made the estate beautiful, she had been its heart. He was as guilty of her death as if he himself had plunged the knife into her throat.

He would have thrown himself howling to the ground in grief, but the sight of Haru approaching made him restrain himself. He hid himself away, unable to face anyone, least of all her.

Haru knelt in front of the smoldering ruin, her eyes not leaving the destruction, her lips moving. There was no sound other than the two werehawks, which from time to time gave their piercing call. The spirits had fallen silent.

A little later two horsemen rode up. He was afraid they might be Aritomo's men, sent back to arrest him, but he saw the black silk coverings over their faces and recognized one of them as Eisei the monk. It was like a hallucination from the past. He remembered that Eisei and the other one similarly disfigured had ridden off with Shikanoko. Did their presence now mean Shikanoko himself was nearby?

The two men dismounted and spoke to Haru. Then they rode away with her. The werehawks followed.

When they had gone he left the pavilion and knelt in Haru's place. He could not decide what to do. It was as though the life force that had animated him had been abruptly shut off. All his ambition, lust, and greed had been reduced to ashes along with his house and his wife. Tama had destroyed him, but he did not resent or hate her for it. He admired her courage more than ever and he knew he had never loved anyone else.

"Forgive me," he whispered. "You were everything to me and I did not know it." Tears burst from his eyes then.

"What should I do?" he said more loudly. He felt the spirits' presence.

"You could kill yourself," came the mocking reply.

"But we don't care if you do or not."

"Live or die, it's all the same to us."

"You no longer matter."

He drew Jinan and laid it on the ground beside him. Last night he had been prepared to take an emperor's life with it. Now he could not even use it against himself. One part of his mind kept niggling at him that he would survive; he always did; he would find a way out. Eventually he decided to listen to it, mainly because he lacked the courage to kill himself.

Jinan: Shikanoko had given it to him, in exchange for Jato, and he had never seen another sword like it. Only its name had displeased him, reminding him as it did of his own status as second son. Yet he was alive and his older brother was dead, just as Aritomo would soon be dead. None of his rules and rituals, his codes for the way of the warrior, his ideals of honor and courage, could save the great lord from the illness that was killing him. *I will outlive them all*, he promised himself. He got to his feet and picked up his sword. The air smelled of smoke and beneath it another stench, as the piles of dead animals began to rot.

"Farewell," he said silently to Tama. He skirted the lake and began to walk along the track in the direction of Kuromori. It was his childhood home; he had lost it and won it back. He would return there and see if anything could be salvaged of his life.

But his spirits failed to recover and he was thinking again of using Jinan to end his life when he heard a twig break, then another, the trample and splash of horses' feet ahead of him. He left the path swiftly and hid himself in the undergrowth.

A group of people on horseback were picking their way along the stream. An ungainly creature ran in the lead, its head swinging from side to side, its nostrils flaring. It was the fake wolf he had seen years ago with Shikanoko. It caught his scent and stopped dead, looking in his direction and growling.

Several horses followed in single file, the first a white black-maned stallion with no bridle, carrying a woman. It halted and neighed loudly. Masachika remembered again his dream about his brother, Kiyoyori, and a foal. He knew it was the same horse, full grown.

A rider on a brown horse pushed past the stallion, dismounted, drew his sword, and approached the bushes where Masachika was concealed.

"Come out and show yourself!" The voice was curiously high, like a woman's.

He came out, his hand on Jinan. Haru spoke from the rear of the line. "It is Masachika."

She rode behind the man with the black face covering

whom he had seen earlier, and Eisei followed them, his ruined face uncovered. Then came Shikanoko himself, on an older white horse, surely the stallion Masachika had found at Nishimi and sent to Ryusonji. He looked back at the black-maned horse and saw the young woman properly. Her expression chilled him to the depths of his being. He felt she saw through him and judged him, and so did the horse. It must be Hina. If she and Shikanoko had come a day earlier, surely Aritomo would have forgiven him everything.

He could hardly bring himself to care. He said, more from habit than any real conviction, "Aritomo has left. He must be taking Yoshimori to the capital. An attack is being launched even now, by sea, on Rakuhara. Take me to Kuromori and I will help you plan a counterattack to rescue the Emperor."

Shikanoko's gaze swept over him. Masachika quailed before the expressionless eyes. Shikanoko said merely, "Ride on," and as the others obeyed, "Ibara! He is yours!"

The black-maned horse gave a loud cry so full of sorrow and anger that Masachika felt another wave of grief engulf him. Within moments all but two of them had disappeared down the track. He called out helplessly, "Shikanoko! I could have helped you. We are on the same side now."

Ibara was the one who had first spoken to Masachika. She was raising her sword. "Go ahead, Mu," she said over her shoulder, to the smaller man who had remained with her. "I don't need you."

"I wouldn't dare suggest you do," the other replied. "But I like to watch you in action, so I'll wait till you've finished."

"It won't take long," the woman said.

"I see you are going to kill me," Masachika said. "You don't know how great a favor you are doing me. But can you tell me why?"

"You don't remember me, do you?"

He searched his memory, but there had been so many women. He had forgotten all their faces, except Tama's.

"My name is Ibara. And the groom you murdered? Have you forgotten him?"

Now he was able to place her. "The man who guided me over the mountains," he said. "You were at Nishimi. You were mad with grief. I spared your life." It seemed almost humorous. He could have killed her then, all those years ago. Now that the end was so near his heart had lightened.

"His name was Saburo," she said, as stern as the lord of Hell in judgment. "We loved each other. You killed him, you caused the death of the Autumn Princess, and because of you my lord, Yukikuni no Takaakira, was forced to take his own life."

The dead crowded around him, clamoring for justice.

"Kill me now," he pleaded. "Be quick!"

"With pleasure," Ibara said.

His eyes were playing tricks on him. It seemed to be Tama standing before him with the sword. He felt profoundly grateful to her. She would punish him and then she would forgive him, be his guide across the three-streamed river of death as she had been in life.

The sword swept. He felt the blow but no pain.

"Tama!" he whispered as he fell.

17

ARITOMO

Once back in Miyako, Aritomo moved swiftly to secure the capital. Every road into it was heavily guarded. His warriors roamed the streets day and night, arresting anyone acting suspiciously and rounding up all those known to have had Kakizuki connections. The imperial lute, Genzo, was locked away. The prisoners were confined in cells in Ryusonji.

He waited anxiously for Masachika, for he was eager to conduct the execution. After several days passed and Masachika still did not return, he began to wonder what could have happened to delay him. Only then did he remember the testament the woman had handed over. He issued orders for it to be brought to him.

He read it in mounting disbelief at all Masachika had concealed from him: Kiyoyori's daughter was alive and was probably Lady Fuji's murderer; Akihime had had a son who also survived. Who were these people, weak and insignificant, women, children, who were undermining his rule? Who were the riverbank people who had concealed them for so long? Their existence was an affront to him. They lived beyond his regulations, they obeyed none of his laws. He set about interrogating and punishing them, starting with Asagao, Masachika's woman who had played the lute. She was only the first of them to die under torture.

It was no great surprise that Masachika had been ready to betray him: he had never trusted him. More unexpected and insulting was the Empress's plan to supplant him. The only thing that comforted him in his shock and rage was his secret: he would outlive them all. What if he did not sleep at night or eat in the day; what if his body seemed to be failing him at the time when he most needed his strength, his flesh melting from his bones; what if when he dozed briefly from exhaustion he was assailed by nightmares? He was not ill; these symptoms were the price to be paid for immortality, the way the body learned to cheat death. He continued to drink the lacquer tea and the water from the well at Ryusonji.

He let a day and a night pass after reading the testament while he reflected on all its implications. Masachika would never come back to the capital. Either he had already killed himself or more likely he had fled. Aritomo vowed to track him down. The Empress and her son would also have to be dealt with, but how would he rebuke them? He would separate them, for a start. The Emperor must move immediately into the new palace. Maybe Lady Natsue could be exiled. Now that Aritomo held Yoshimori, she would have to stop her ridiculous plotting against him.

Arinori's name had been mentioned several times in the interrogations, as the protector of Lady Yayoi, who had turned out to be Kiyoyori's daughter, the one who had found her at the temple and procured the privilege of being her first lover. Aritomo longed to question him, but Arinori had sailed to the west, leading the attack against the Kakizuki. No word had come from him. Aritomo did not believe the surprise attack could fail; he was impatient to hear of the annihilation of his enemies. But troubling signs began to manifest themselves.

Late the following afternoon when he went to Ryusonji a white dove inexplicably dropped dead from the sky, in front of his horse, feathers fluttering after it like miniature Miboshi banners. As he crossed a bridge, he heard a voice say, distinctly, "The white one is spoiled. Chuck it away." In the cloister he heard another voice, accompanied by a lute, singing a ballad about the fall of the Miboshi and the return of Kiyoyori.

It was Sesshin, whom Aritomo had had confined in a room in his own palace. Wondering how he had escaped, he told two of his men to bring the old man to him. They returned, one of them carrying the lute, the other holding Sesshin by the arm. Sesshin again seemed to have forgotten who Aritomo was.

"What did those words mean?" Aritomo demanded. "Were they a prophecy?"

"The past and the future are one," Sesshin mumbled.

"Sometimes I sing of one, sometimes of another. But where's my lute?"

He rambled for a while in a way no one understood, before beginning to sing again.

The dragon's child
Sleeps in the lake.
Where is his father?
Where is his sister?
When the deer's child calls
He will awaken.

He broke off suddenly and sniffed the air. "Someone is very ill. Someone is dying. But where's my lute? Who stole my lute?"

"I am not dying," Aritomo said in fury. "I am like you; I will live forever. Break the lute! Destroy it!"

"Shall we kill him, lord?" asked one of the warriors, while the other smashed the lute against a column and then stamped on it.

"No!" he replied, seized by superstitious fear. "Send him away. Banish him. Let me never hear his voice again."

He did not wait to be announced to Lady Natsue, but burst into her apartment, pushing her ladies aside and ordering them to leave.

She sat immobile, outraged, indicating with her head that he should bow. When he did not her eyes flashed in anger. She said in an icy voice, "I must congratulate Lord Aritomo. You have found Yoshimori. You have achieved all

I asked of you. But why do you delay any further? You must execute him at once."

"I will," he said, and then, "Your Majesty should know that you will not see the Matsutani lord, Masachika, again."

She went still and lowered her gaze.

"I don't expect him to show his face in the capital, but if he does he, too, will be executed. I don't have to tell you why, but we will not discuss it further."

When she said nothing, he went on. "I will not be overthrown."

She sat in silence for several moments, only a faint flush at her neck revealing her rage. Then she said, "Where are the werehawks?"

"The werehawks?" he repeated. "They flew away."

"They should have flown straight back to Ryusonji, if you were unable to win their obedience. One werehawk has returned, but it is older and has some gold feathers. It sits on the roof above the prisoners' cells and calls in an intolerable way. The other two must have gone to someone else—the only person who could control them is the one who destroyed my brother, the deer's child, Shikanoko. You will not be safe until he is dead."

Sesshin's song came back to him: *When the deer's child calls / He will awaken.*

"Shikanoko will come here," Aritomo said. "And I will be ready for him. I have no more to say to you now. You will have to move away from the capital. I will inform you where that is to be. Let your son know this: his position is upheld by me. He may be the Emperor, but I hold all the power."

Dusk was falling as he left. He saw the werehawk keeping watch on the roof and could not resist the impulse to listen to the prisoners, hungry to know all he could of Yoshimori before he put an end to his life. He told his men to go on to the gate and went silently to the outside of the cell.

At first there was only silence, then he heard one, not Yoshimori, the other one, whose name he had been told was something ridiculous like Sarumaru, say, "It's true, isn't it? You really are the Emperor?"

"No!" Yoshimori said. "It's all a mistake."

"Then why does the lute play for you?" Saru demanded.

"I don't know," Yoshimori said quietly.

"Don't lie to me," the other exclaimed. "Not after all we have been to each other. I was there on the boat when we pulled Yayoi and Take from the water. It played then. And that crazy bird, Kon, that's why it follows you, isn't it? Where did you come from?"

"I hardly remember," Yoshimori said. "I know a young woman took me away from a burning palace and told me to pretend I was someone else. But before that, everything is confused. I don't know if it is a memory or a dream. I was carried everywhere—I wanted to run, but the women wouldn't let me. My father was addressed as Prince, my mother as Princess, but my real life, the one I do remember, only began shortly before I met you in the Darkwood."

"None of it matters since they are going to kill us," Saru said.

"Let's pray together," Yoshimori whispered, and he

began the words of a prayer Aritomo had never heard before. He shuffled closer to the door.

"Someone's coming!" Saru cried. "Are they going to take us out and execute us now?"

Aritomo froze. After a long silence he heard Yoshimori say quietly, "The Secret One is with us, just as the priest always told us. He will never forsake us."

"But if you are the Emperor," Saru said, sniffing as if through tears, "you are descended from the gods. You are divine!"

"I don't dare think that about myself," Yoshimori replied.

"Why are we forbidden to kill when all around us the beasts kill each other, men slaughter them in their hundreds, like in the great hunt we witnessed, and think nothing of taking human life? Even animals fight for their lives. If we were not forbidden to fight we could defend ourselves. A cornered rat has more courage than we have."

"All living beings fear death," Yoshimori said. "That's why we should not inflict it on any of them. I suppose you are sorry that you found me in the forest? I am more sorry than I can say, for causing this suffering to you and all our friends."

"I would die to save your life," Saru said. "You know that, don't you? Didn't I pretend to be you, when we were first seized? I would even kill to save you."

"Better to leave it all in the hands of the Secret One," Yoshimori said.

"I am not sure I believe in that god any longer," Saru said in an anguish-filled voice.

"At least Kai is safe," Yoshi said very quietly. "That must be part of his plan, for if she had not been carrying our child she would have come with us. I don't fear my own death, but I dread hers."

The silence deepened over the temple. The musicians had quietened. No one sang; no one screamed. It was almost raining. A dank drizzle filled the air, and the eaves dripped with moisture. The bird called from the roof, startling Aritomo.

"That's Kon!" Saru said suddenly. "It's still around. Why doesn't it go for help?"

"I don't think anyone can help us now," Yoshimori said.

Aritomo waited for a long time, but neither of them spoke again. He returned to his palace deeply disturbed by all he had heard. The bird might go for help? Help from whom? Kiyoyori's daughter? Shikanoko? Yoshimori and the other acrobats belonged to some hitherto unknown sect? He had an unborn child? Was Aritomo going to have to scour the Eight Islands all over again to find another supposed heir to the throne?

Messengers came that night, two of them, faces ashen with fear. Aritomo had the reputation of summarily executing bearers of bad news. There had been a sea battle. The Kakizuki had been forewarned. Arinori's fleet had sailed into a trap, carried by the tide into the waiting warships. He was dead and most of his men drowned, the ships sent to the bottom of the Encircled Sea. Shortly after, others came from the opposite direction, from the east. Yukikuni no Takauji was in open rebellion and was laying siege to Minatogura.

"The pretender, Yoshimori, dies tomorrow," Aritomo declared. Vomit rose in his throat and he tried to hold it down but could not. Pain tore through him. For a moment he thought savagely that the messengers' deaths would ease it, but then he reminded himself he would need every man he had. The Kakizuki would certainly attempt to return to the capital. He must prepare an army to counteract and surprise them. But whom could he trust, now that Arinori and Masachika were gone? Someone had betrayed his plans. There must be spies everywhere. He groaned loudly.

His attendants tried to persuade him to rest, but he could not lie down with any ease. He was dressed and ready before dawn, and as he paced the floor waiting for daybreak he heard the steady splash of water from the eaves, a sound so unfamiliar for a moment he did not recognize it.

The Emperor is in the capital and it is raining.

18

HINA

Hina stood beside Tan in front of the west gate at Matsutani. It was the only part of the building still intact; the house, the pavilions, the stables and other outbuildings were smouldering ruins, charred wood, ash that was once thatch.

In their niche, among the carvings, the eyes gleamed. She had not seen them since she had left them at Nishimi, when she had fled all those years ago with Take.

"They are Sesshin's eyes, Father," she murmured to Kiyoyori's spirit. She had fallen into the habit of telling him everything, and even when she did not put her thoughts into words, she felt he understood them. "Do you remember when we found them on the ground after the earthquake? They make you see yourself as you really are, not as you wish you were."

Ibara rode up behind her and dismounted. She said to Hina, "It is done. Masachika is dead."

The horse shuddered slightly and bowed its head three times.

"So soon after my stepmother died," Hina said. "In the end they were not parted for long. May they find peace together and be reborn into a better life."

"You are more forgiving than me, Lady Hina. I don't know enough about her, but I hope he rots in Hell!"

Ibara's breath caught in her throat and then she said, "Revenge is not as sweet as I thought it would be. Why should I feel regret and pity now, for all his mistakes and my own?"

"It is the eyes," Hina said. "Under their gaze, you see yourself without the armor of your self-regard, and in that light you can only feel regret, remorse, and pity."

Tan bowed his head and nuzzled her shoulder.

It was late afternoon, the sky was covered in clouds, and the air felt damp as though rain might fall at any moment. Nagatomo and Eisei had fashioned torches from burning wood.

Shikanoko called to them, "We must ride on. If the spirits have returned to the gateposts, let them remain there. Nothing is left for them to destroy. Aritomo and Yoshimori are more than a day ahead of us. We have no time to waste."

Hina thought she heard a whisper.

"Shikanoko is here!"

"I heard his voice, didn't you?"

"I did! I heard his voice!"

Hina wondered aloud, "Should I bring the eyes?" There was nothing left for them to keep watch over and it seemed fitting that they should be with the Kudzu Vine Treasure Store and the medicine stone that she carried in her bag.

Tan nodded vigorously.

"I don't have anything to put them in," Hina said.

"Here." Ibara handed her a small bamboo box, empty apart from some scarlet maple leaves. "I like to pick the leaves up, sometimes, I don't know why. Shake them out if you want to."

"No," Hina replied. "They will make a fine mat to put the eyes on."

She vaulted onto Tan's back to reach them, and as she lifted them down and placed them carefully in the box she heard a voice say, more loudly, "Who's that?"

"It must be Kiyoyori's daughter!"

"Lady! Lady! You are back!"

"Welcome home!"

"Is Kiyoyori with her?"

"I feel he is, don't you?"

Shikanoko, a werehawk on each shoulder, rode up to the gate, calling her name. "Lady Hina, are you ready?"

"Shikanoko!" the first voice cried.

"I knew it was you," said the second.

"You have both been misbehaving again," Shikanoko said sternly. "You have destroyed the very place you were meant to guard. I should shut you up in a rock for a thousand years!"

"We didn't mean to."

"Everything was so out of kilter and amiss."

"Yes, amiss and awry and out of kilter."

"The Emperor was here."

"They were going to kill him."

"So we saved his life, you see."

"Then I forgive you and I bid you farewell," Shikanoko said. "Come, Lady Hina, Ibara."

Hina sat on Tan's back and put the bamboo box in her bag. Ibara leaped onto her horse and called to Mu to join her.

"Don't leave us here!" one of the spirits cried.

"No, don't leave us here. Take us with you."

"You belong here. Your master, Sesshin, placed you here," Shikanoko said.

"There is nothing to guard here anymore."

"We want to come with you."

"How will you travel?" Shikanoko asked. "You cannot just waft around disembodied for that length of time. I would need to put you in something."

"I want to go in your sword."

"No, I want to go in the sword."

"I said it first, you choose something else."

"I'll go in the bow."

"No!" Shikanoko said. "I don't want you in either my sword or my bow. I would never be able to rely on either of them again."

"We will behave."

"We promise."

"We will protect you. Your sword will be the strongest."

"Your bow, the most accurate."

"Oh, very well," Shikanoko said. "I don't have time to argue now."

He spoke a word of power. The air shimmered. Both Jato and Kodama took on a sudden glow as if they were lit from within. It faded slowly.

"And no chattering," Shikanoko said, as he clicked his tongue to Nyorin to move forward.

"We'll be completely silent."

"As silent as the grave."

They had ridden a little way when Shikanoko called to Ibara to ride alongside Nyorin so he could talk to Mu.

"You said Kiku had offered to help us. We'll need him, but we have no way of getting in touch with him in time."

"We'll ride with your message," Ibara said eagerly.

"It takes days to get to Kitakami and then back to the capital," Shikanoko replied.

"I wish I could summon up a tengu or fly myself," said Mu. "What about those birds? Can you send them?"

"They are young and untrained. I don't think they are reliable." The birds croaked indignantly at him, one in each ear. "They are eager to go, but even if they find their way, Kiku might not understand them. Worse, he might kill them, as you and he did Gessho's."

"Send a sign with them; send the little fawn I gave you. Kiku will know the birds come from you. I'm sure he will be able to talk to them."

"I suppose we must try it." Shika took the carved fawn from the breast of his robe, pulled out a thread from the material, and tied the tiny figure to the larger bird's leg.

"Go," he said. "Fly north. I will guide you with my mind."

As the birds fluttered away he said to Mu, "I have never done this before. I don't even know if it is possible."

Most of the way they rode in single file, with Nyorin leading, but Tan also liked to be in front, and when the track widened, he pushed his way forward to canter alongside his father.

Despite being side by side, Shikanoko and Hina still hardly spoke. Sometimes she felt there was a depth of understanding between them, at other times he seemed remote and distant. Once or twice she caught him looking at her, with a kind of longing that made her heart jump with hope, but then he seemed to withdraw within himself, assuming his cold, distant demeanor.

As they came closer to Miyako they realized the roads were heavily guarded. Shikanoko decided to ride through the mountains, making their journey longer. Six days after they left Matsutani, they came out of the woods and saw the capital spread out below them. From that distance it looked as it always did, giving no sign that the Emperor was present or that he was alive.

The air was damp and cool. Around them the trees were in full color, made more radiant by the dim light. They were not far from the eastern bank of the river, hidden by the thick woods that covered the slope of the mountain. Across the river, which had shrunk to a trickle during the years of drought, could be seen the five-storied pagoda of

Ryusonji and the cedar-shingled roofs of its great halls. The temple bell sounded the sunset hour, its sonorous tone echoing from the surrounding hills and followed by other bells throughout the city.

Despite the hour and the rain, the riverbank swarmed with people. Their clothes were brightly colored, glowing in the dusk. Some curious trick of the evening light brought out all the red and orange hues.

"It's the riverbank people," Hina said. "From the boats."

"They have come to watch," Take said beside her, his face riven with anxiety. "We are going to rescue him, Yoshi, the Emperor? We are going to be in time?"

"Yes, tomorrow we will rescue him," Shikanoko promised.

Mu and Ibara found a spring, lit a small, smokeless fire, and boiled water. Ibara washed the mud from the horses' legs and Hina took her beechwood comb and untangled Tan's mane and tail, brushing them out with her fingers. Then she did the same for Nyorin. The horses, father and son, stood as still as carvings, nose to nose, only their nostrils quivering as they exchanged breath.

Take disappeared with Nagatomo and Eisei and returned with two squirrels and a rabbit. Hina drank a little warm water, but refused food. There was some shelter under a ledge of rock and Shikanoko suggested she rest there.

"What about you?" she said. His clothes were already dark with moisture.

"I will stay awake. I have not told the others, but I lost contact with the werehawks. I don't know where they are or if they ever got to Kitakami. I must make one last effort to find them."

"Then I will stay awake with you."

He bowed formally to her and went a little way away, under a spreading yew whose thickly leaved branches gave some protection. She saw him remove his sword and bow and place them beside him, speaking a few words to them, and then giving each one a light pat. Then he drew his legs up under him and closed his eyes.

She closed hers. She heard the others whispering for a while. A night bird made a sudden jarring call. In the distance dogs were barking. Gen whimpered in response.

Hina's mind was empty for a long time. Then a waking dream came over her. She was riding Tan across the river. Someone waited for her there. She had never seen him, but she knew it was Lord Aritomo. She saw his disease revealed, the rotting lungs, the decaying bones.

I have to take the medicine stone to him to show him he is dying.

She opened her eyes and looked at where Shikanoko sat. It was very dark. The fire had almost died down; only the embers gleamed. She thought he had put on the mask, thought she saw the outline of the antlers, but then she realized it was only shadows. There was a slight reflection from Gen's gemstone eyes.

Slowly the sky paled. While it was still the gray half-light just before dawn, Shikanoko stood and walked to her. Kneeling beside her, he said, "I saw you showing something to Lord Aritomo."

"I saw it, too. It seems I must take the medicine stone to him."

"What's that?"

"It's something your mother gave to me."

"My mother? When did you meet my mother?"

Hina wanted to tell him everything, but there was no time. She was gripped by fear that there would never be time, that they would die that day, before they had really spoken to each other. All she said now was "She asked you to forgive her."

"Is she still alive? Where is she?"

"She died, but she saw Takeyoshi before she passed away; we were both by her side."

His mouth closed in a tight line. He seemed to hold his breath for a long time before letting it out in a deep sigh.

"You must give me a full account after everything is over," he said, so distant again. "Let me see the stone."

Hina drew it from the bag and held it out to him. He took it and looked curiously at it.

"It does not seem to be either precious or beautiful. Is it anything more than a rock?"

"If you are sick, it shows you if you will die or if you will recover," Hina explained. "It helped me read the Kudzu Vine Treasure Store. It is a tool in diagnosis and healing."

"Does it reveal the time of one's death?" he said, peering closely in to it.

"If that time is close, it does."

"Well, I see nothing," he said, laughing as his mood changed swiftly. "But I hope Aritomo will. We will ride side by side and show it to him."

"I should go alone," she said. "I will be able to approach him."

"Lady Hina, I would obey you in everything, but not in this. I will be at your side."

The light was strengthening. From across the river came the werehawk's frantic call. Tan neighed loudly in response. Shikanoko ran to the edge of the trees and looked down.

He called back to the others, "Aritomo has arrived! We can't wait any longer."

Nagatomo was already preparing the horses. Shikanoko held out his hands. His bow flew into his right hand, his sword into his left.

"Thank you," he said to the spirits. "Now behave yourselves, I am depending on you!" Smiling a little, he turned to Hina. "Are you ready, lady?"

Tan stood beside her, quivering with excitement. She put the stone back in the bag and tied it to her waist. Shikanoko lifted her onto Tan's back. The horse's coat was as smooth as silk beneath her fingers; the black mane she had combed out the night before fell over his neck like a woman's hair.

Shikanoko swung himself up onto Nyorin. "Wait out of sight," he said to the others. "If we all appear at once, the guards will shoot as soon as we are within range."

"And they won't shoot at you two?" Nagatomo said. "You are riding into certain death!"

"I am counting on Aritomo's curiosity," Shikanoko replied. "If Heaven does not protect me now, then I'll know I faced its just punishment."

"Let me go with you, Father," Take begged.

Shikanoko looked at him with an expression of tenderness. "If I die," he said to Nagatomo, "you and Eisei must escape with my son and serve him as you have served me. Go to the east, to Takauji."

"We will, lord," they promised, bowing their heads.

The temple gardens at Ryusonji spread around the lake, where the dragon's child slept, down to the riverbank. The walls had once run down to the water's edge, too, but now the water had receded so much there was a wide gap on either side. Guards, armed with spears, had been placed here to keep back the throng of people who had been gathering since the previous night, drawn by rumors and premonitions that they were going to witness the execution of an emperor.

It was misty, drizzling slightly, and the crowd was silent, with somber, expectant faces.

Aritomo himself, hollow-eyed and stern, sat on a platform hastily erected in the garden between the lake and the river. A ginkgo tree nearby was shedding its golden leaves, and maples glowed red. Butterbur flowers were a brilliant yellow around rocks and at the foot of stone lanterns. The paths among the moss were raked smooth. The temple bell tolled the hour of sunrise.

The two white horses emerged out of the mist, picking their way through the shallows, the splashing of their feet louder than the flow of the river. A guard broke away from the others and ran toward them, shouting at the riders to stay back.

Hina thought she heard voices whispering, "Shikanoko! It is Shikanoko!"

Aritomo rose to his feet. "Seize them! They will be executed along with the pretender."

She took the medicine stone from her bag and held it aloft. "I have a gift for Lord Aritomo. It will reveal life and death to him."

Her clear voice could be heard throughout the gardens. There was a murmur of surprise from the crowd. Aritomo, momentarily distracted, said, "Let her come to me."

Shikanoko dismounted and walked forward, the two stallions following him closely.

Aritomo called, "Put down your weapons!"

Shikanoko took the sword from his sash and the bow from his shoulder and laid them down on the moss, along with his quiver. He lifted Hina from Tan and they both fell to their knees a few paces away from the platform.

Hina was aware that death might come at any moment, yet in that instant of vulnerability she felt no fear, only a sense of rightness, of being exactly where she was meant to be, in this early morning of the tenth month, in the hour of the hare.

Aritomo made a sign to one of his attendants, who stepped down from the platform and approached Hina. He reached out to take the stone, but she stood swiftly and said, "It is for Lord Aritomo's eyes only."

The man looked back to Aritomo. The Minatogura lord, his curiosity piqued, said, "Let her bring it to me."

Hina stepped onto the platform and held out the medicine stone. Aritomo looked at it warily, and then looked into her face.

"It will show you if you are to live or die," she said. "Take it and look into it. If Heaven wills it, you will know how to prepare yourself."

She saw the naked longing in his face, so intense it brought on a bout of coughing. As he struggled to get his breath, it was clear to Hina, even without the aid of the stone, that his illness was mortal. She watched him with calm compassion. He was a mighty lord, a general, a warrior, the most powerful man in the Eight Islands, but, like everything else, he was destined to die.

He took the stone in both hands and looked into it. His face took on an even more deathly hue.

"I am dying?" he whispered to her.

"The stone does not lie," she replied.

His fingers gripped it with white knuckles as he stared at his own death. Then he lowered the stone and for a few moments sat speechless. She saw the struggle within him: part of him longed for peace so he might prepare himself for death, but his iron will would not allow him to deviate from the path he had set.

"It is a lie," he cried. "I am not dying. I am immortal. I cannot die. But let Yoshimori look in it and see his imminent death!"

The stone in his hands gleamed as bright and dazzling as a mirror.

"Bring out the imposter!" Aritomo ordered. "I will see him dead and then deal with this witch and Shikanoko."

Hina was seized, dragged off the platform, and thrown to the ground.

Guards appeared immediately, as though they had been nervously awaiting this command, Yoshi walking between them. He had been dressed in a robe of rough hemp cloth, a dirty brown color. His hands were bound behind his back, his feet were bare. Hina stared first at his face, in which she thought she saw both resignation and fear. His eyes glanced once around. She thought he saw her but could not be sure. Would he recognize Shikanoko?

He stared up at the mountains and the ragged white clouds that hung around them. His lips moved as if he were praying. A slight smile crossed his face. Following his gaze, Hina saw Kon circling overhead, screeching wildly. Yoshi lowered his eyes, and Hina looked at his feet. The long, flexible toes gripped the earth, as though at any moment they would launch him into an acrobatic show. But where were the others? Saru, the monkeys? Surely they were not all already dead?

Yoshi was forced to his knees. An even deeper hush fell over the spectators. Hina could not believe it was truly going to happen. She could not prevent herself from sitting up and looking around, seeking help.

Aritomo stepped down from the platform and went to Yoshimori. "Look into this," he said, holding out the stone. "See that you are about to die!"

The Emperor of the Eight Islands looked at the stone, then looked at Aritomo, his face calm.

Light flashed from the stone. Aritomo dropped it as though it had become red hot and took a step back.

"Now!" he said. "Do it now!"

Hina heard the sigh of a sword being raised. A sob burst from her.

Kon swooped down, flew around the raised sword, and

stabbed the executioner in the eye. Tan gave a fierce neigh like a human scream and charged at the man. He stumbled and rolled on the ground but kept a firm grip on the sword and, as the horse reared over him, thrust upward, deep into Tan's chest.

"Tan!" Hina screamed. "Father!"

She heard Aritomo shouting to his warriors. "Kill them all, horses and all. Don't let any of them escape."

Blood was staining the white silken hair. Tan lowered his head, fell to his knees. Hardly knowing how she had got there, Hina found herself next to him, trying in vain to stanch the wound. The horse's body seemed to melt and fade and in its place stood her father, young and courageous, just as she had last seen him when she was a child. Kiyoyori held out his hand and the sword Jato flew to him from where it lay on the moss.

Shika called to Kodama, "Come here!" and the bow launched itself into the air, along with the arrows. As soon as he held them he shot twice rapidly at Aritomo. Both arrows found their mark, one in the neck, one in the chest, but the Minatogura lord was impervious to pain or fear. With raised sword he rushed at the kneeling Emperor.

"Lord Kiyoyori!" Shika shouted.

"I cannot die!" Aritomo cried. "Not one of you can kill me."

"I am returned from the dead," the warrior replied. "I can kill you. It is for this that I was called back by Shika-noko." He let Jato move with its lightning speed to cut the sword from Aritomo's hand and with the returning stroke slash him from shoulder to hip, sending him to his knees.

Aritomo struggled to his feet. Nothing was going to kill him. He stood for a long moment, even as his life's blood ebbed from him. Then with a cry of despair and disbelief, he fell heavily into the mud, quivered, and lay still.

Kiyoyori lowered the sword, went to Hina, and took her in his arms.

"Father," Hina said again, with sorrow, for she knew he was about to leave her, this time forever.

"My work is done," Kiyoyori said. "Don't weep for me, my brave daughter."

He handed Jato back to Shika and said, "Thank you, Shikanoko. All debts between us are settled."

Yoshi still knelt on the ground, Kon on his shoulder.

"Jato, we may need to fight now," Shika said quietly, looking at Aritomo's men, who, shocked and enraged by the death of their lord, were gathering around them. "This is your true emperor," he cried to them. "Lay down your weapons and surrender to him!"

When none of them obeyed, Kiyoyori called toward the lake. "Come, Tsumaru, my son! I am ready to join you!"

There was a sound like a thunderclap and a crackle of flame. A cloud of steam rolled over them. The lake was boiling. Some said, afterward, they saw the dragon child, with its wings and its talons, its ruby red eyes, take Kiyoyori's spirit in its embrace and descend with him into the lake, where father and son would dwell together until the end of time. Hina believed it was true. But she herself saw nothing until the steam cleared. Aritomo lay dead; his warriors milled to and fro, unsure whether to flee or to fight or to surrender; the crowd was running away; werehawks circled overhead, crying in triumph. Down the river, from the north, came an army like nothing she had ever seen before. Warriors with one eye, with wooden legs, with hooks in place of hands, the Crippled Army, and at their head, riding on a black horse, a man who resembled Mu as closely as a twin. The guards who had not run away already tried to do so now, but for most of them it was too late.

Shikanoko went to Yoshi, loosened his hands, raised him to his feet, then knelt before him, offering him Jato.

"Your Majesty may now safely ascend the Lotus Throne," he said in a loud voice that echoed around Ryusonji. Kon fluttered down in front of them, calling exultantly.

"I don't want your sword," Yoshi said. "I don't want to be Emperor. You can't make me. I would rather be dead!"

As if in response rain began to fall heavily.

19

SHIKANOKO

"It has nothing to do with whether you want it or not," Shika-noko said, making no attempt to hide his exasperation. It was a cold day in early winter. It seemed he had made the same argument a hundred times. Yoshimori had been moved to the luxurious palace that had been built for Daigen, and clothed in robes befitting an emperor, but he still refused to start acting as one. "You were born into this position, by the will of Heaven. The whole land, all the Eight Islands, depends on you. It's not possible for you to refuse it."

"There must be someone else, someone who actually wants to be Emperor," Yoshi said. "What about the one who was ruling before I was discovered?"

"The former Emperor Daigen has been sent into exile," Shika said, "along with his mother and his household. He may never return to Miyako, but he will not be ill treated."

Kuro and Kiku had offered to get rid of him, but Shika

had forbidden it and had sent Daigen away before the brothers could dispatch him in the way they had the women and children at Kumayama.

"Does that mean you had him killed?" Yoshi said, eyeing Shika with mistrust. "And you will have me killed, when I become an inconvenience."

"I swear he is alive. As for you, you are the son of Heaven. I offered my sword, Jato, to you. I will serve you for the rest of my life."

"As I said, I don't want your sword," said Yoshi. "I gave it to Take."

When Shika merely bowed in response, Yoshi said, "If I did agree to become emperor my first imperial command would be to send you into exile!"

"If that is to be the price, I will pay it," Shika replied. Yoshimori had threatened this in previous conversations, and exile was beginning to look more and more attractive. Quite apart from Yoshi's stubbornness, life in the capital, as the Kakizuki returned to take up power again and Kiku and his Crippled Army demanded recognition and rewards for their part in the victory, became more complicated every day. Everyone came to him with requests, demands, threats, promises. Lord Keita was reputed to be on his way back from Rakuhara and his old palace was being restored to all its former luxury. Minatogura had fallen to Takauji, who had declared his loyalty to the true emperor and wrote asking for advice on how to subdue and administer the port city.

Aritomo and his warriors had to be buried with all the appropriate ceremonies lest their enraged spirits return to haunt the capital.

Hina and Ibara were living in Lord Kiyoyori's old house, but Shika had not visited them, had not seen Hina since the day of Aritomo's death. He told himself he had been too busy, but he was not sure of his own feelings, and besides, what did he have to offer her? It was clear that she loved him, for she had been able to break the spell of the mask, but what could he do about it if he was under threat of banishment?

Who am I? he had often thought during the sleepless nights as autumn turned to winter. *Who is this person, a grown man, to whom they defer as if he knows what is right and what to do next?* He had lived for years in the forest. He knew nothing of the administration of cities, of the entire country. He saw people turn to him, but they were afraid of him. He remembered the promise of the mask. Should he take up residence at Ryusonji and become another Prince Abbot, practicing that sacred sorcery that protected the realm? Or was his calling to be like Kiyoyori, a warrior lord, a great general, defeating the Emperor's enemies, pacifying the outer islands, repelling invaders? Everything was possible to him, yet without Yoshimori's trust and cooperation he could do nothing.

"Your life will not be unpleasant," he said now to Yoshimori. "You will never lack anything, never be hungry again. I've been told you are very fond of women—you will have all the concubines you want, the most beautiful girls in the realm, or boys if you prefer. You will marry a princess."

"What if I told you I was already married?" Yoshi said. "I don't want any other woman, I want only her."

"I am not sure she would be considered suitable," Shika said.

"Then I will never be emperor," Yoshi replied.

"Maybe she could be included among your concubines," Shika suggested.

Yoshi gave him a look of contempt as if this was not even worth answering.

"In any case, I won't be able to roam in the forest with Saru and the monkeys, will I?" he said finally.

"A forest can be put aside for you and filled with monkeys, I suppose," Shika said. "And Saru can join you wherever you like. He can be given a noble rank." He had discovered that Saru was the youngest brother of Taro, who had taken Kiyoyori's place on the ferry across the river of death. Saru deserved some reward for his brother's sacrifice. "Where is he now?"

"He is here in the palace recovering. But he wants to go back to Aomizu with the other acrobats, those who survived. If only I were free to go with them!"

"None of us is free," Shika said. "We are all constrained by ties of duty, loyalty, service. You are bound to Heaven, I am bound to you, and so it goes throughout the realm."

"On the riverbank I was free," Yoshimori replied. "We all were. You should know this, you lived in the Darkwood like a wild animal for years, doing as you pleased, obeying no one."

Shika did not reply for a few moments, thinking of the Darkwood, of the pleasures and suffering he had experienced there, of all its creatures, both real and magical.

"I was less free there than I am now," he said finally. "I was trapped, half man and half stag, imprisoned by another's sorcery and my own guilt and grief." He took a deep breath and said, "I suppose we must face what took place all those years ago." It was painful, but he would do anything to obtain reconciliation between them.

"You were going to kill me," Yoshimori said. "I have never spoken of it to anyone, but I have never forgotten it. I was only six years old and you were going to kill me."

"I deeply regret it, all of it. I have spent years atoning for it. I can only ask you to forgive me."

"I should," Yoshimori said, with feeling. "We are taught to forgive. But since we are being honest I will tell you I cannot. It is a gut feeling, as strong as anything I have ever felt. I cannot bear your presence. I do not even want to look at you."

Shikanoko said nothing, feeling more alone than he ever had in his life. He could not help recalling the night he had spent with Akihime, his forbidden passion, the grief and guilt he had lived with since. He had been under the control of another's will, had been outplayed by the Prince Abbot, had come close to killing Yoshimori. He still ached from the punishment Kon and the horses had meted out to him.

They forgave me, he thought now. *But it seems Yoshimori never will.*

"Heaven saved your life then," he pleaded. "Surely that is an indication of its plans for you?"

Yoshimori's expression changed again. "When you and

I talk of Heaven we mean different things," he said slowly. "Your world is full of sorcery and darkness, revenge, conquest, and death. Your Heaven is implacable and unfathomable. But I want to live in another kingdom, one where there is no killing, where Heaven is merciful. To rule as emperor I must accept that I am divine, the son of the gods, yet I believe that only the Secret One can be divine, and we are all equal, all his children. I cannot set myself up above others or above him. I don't expect you to understand. It's how I was brought up, how I've lived till now. It could be argued that that was my destiny."

Shika had noticed that Yoshimori would eat only vegetables and bean curd. Take had told him a little about the sect to which the acrobats belonged. It had not seemed of any great importance. Now he saw that for Yoshi it was.

"If you want the court to stop eating meat, it is within your power to do so," he said. "You have only to express a desire and it will be carried out. You have experienced life in a way few other emperors have. You have the knowledge and the power to do great good for your people."

"And if I ordered you to stop all killing, would that be carried out, too?"

"No one should take another's life lightly," Shikanoko said. "But men will always fight to defend themselves and their families; the evil need to be kept in check, the wicked punished, the realm protected. The warrior class serves you in this respect, my son and I first among them."

"There is no point talking to you," Yoshimori said. "I will never be able to make you understand. But you cannot force me against my will."

Shika knew it was true. He was the Emperor. No one could force him to do anything, not even to become emperor.

He left the hall and walked down a long passage, as courtiers on either side bowed deeply to him. On the veranda he paused to breathe and recover his equilibrium. Being with Yoshimori, feeling the strength of the younger man's dislike, distressed him beyond words. The sky was covered by low gray clouds. The wind was icy and damp. He thought he could smell snow in it. The last of the leaves had fallen. Gardeners were gathering them into piles. On one side of the step grew an ancient kumquat tree, its fruit forming, tiny and green.

Yoshimori must ascend the throne before it ripens, he vowed.

Take was waiting for him at the gate with Nyorin, and the brown horse that had been Chika's. He wore the sword Jato at his hip and the bow Ameyumi on his back, and carried Shika's bow, Kodama, and quiver, and Jinan, which had been recovered after Masachika's death.

Kon perched on the roof of the gate. The two young werehawks were sitting on Nyorin's back. They flapped their wings and cried in excitement at Shika's approach.

"How is he?" Take asked.

"As stubborn as ever. Between you and me I don't think I will ever persuade him. I did not realize his religion would be such a hindrance. You were brought up with the acrobats, do you share his beliefs?"

"Not really," Take admitted. "I admire them, but I can't keep them myself. I like swords and fighting and eating meat."

His honest response made Shika smile. "And the young woman he calls his wife, tell me more about her."

"She is beautiful, clever, and kind," Take said, a light coming into his eyes. Shika wondered if he was not a bit in love with her himself. He would soon be old enough to marry.

"He shouldn't have to give her up," Shika said.

"Her ears are not like other people's," Take explained. "They say it's a blemish."

"I suppose that would be a problem for the Imperial Household. They have many arcane regulations and requirements that have to be followed."

"I'm not surprised Yoshi doesn't want to be emperor," Take said. "I would hate it."

The horses picked their way through the refuse-filled streets. Shika began to think about the problems of cleaning up the capital. The river was flowing freely again, but so many people had fled, there was no one left to do menial work, and when he had suggested to Tsunetomo that the Crippled Army might help, he had been met with incredulous laughter.

"We may be cripples, but we are still warriors," Tsunetomo said. "We will never do the work of refuse collectors."

Take was also silent, as if preoccupied by something he did not know how to put into words. Finally he said, "Father, you should take your sword back. It doesn't feel right that I should wear it."

"I gave it to the Emperor and he gave it to you. It's yours now, and will be your son's."

"I'm not sure that I can control it. Last night it danced for a long time around midnight and today when I went to pick it up it wriggled beneath my fingers like a snake."

"It is Hidarisama misbehaving," Shika said. He had been meaning to deal with the guardian spirits but had been so concerned with everything else, he had not yet had the opportunity.

"Let's ride to Ryusonji," he said. "I will find something there for them to look after."

As they approached the temple Shika heard the strains of singing. Ahead of them on the long avenue that led to the main gate, a figure walked in a wavering, stumbling fashion. The werehawks squawked and cackled and flew to circle above his head, and then back to Shikanoko.

"It is a poor blind man," Take said. "He must be lost."

He leaped down from his horse and went to the man's side, speaking clearly. "Sir. Let me guide you. Where is it you want to go?"

The blind man replied in a surprisingly strong voice, "I am on my way back to Ryusonji. Someone has to keep an eye on the Book of the Future. Aritomo sent me far away, but he couldn't send me far enough!"

Shika recognized the voice and at the same time felt the bow on his back shudder and heard a whisper.

"It is our old master."

The response came from Jato's direction. "Now we're in trouble."

"He'll be angry, won't he?"

"He'll be furious."

Shika dismounted and went to Sesshin. "Master," he said. "It is I, Shikanoko."

Sesshin turned toward his voice. "Is that really you, my boy? It's taken you long enough to get here. And why have you brought those rascals with you? They should be at Matsutani."

"There's nothing left there," said Hidarisama.

"Was I talking to you? Silence!"

"It all burned down," Migisama muttered.

"Silence, I said. I will deal with you later."

"I hope to find somewhere for them at Ryusonji," Shika said.

"Good idea. They'll have to behave then." Sesshin began to hum and then resumed the song he had been singing before,

At the temple of Ryusonji
Where the dragon child dwells
With his father, Kiyoyori . . .

He broke off to say, "You know Kiyoyori dwells there now, too?"

"I suppose his work on earth was complete." Shikanoko thought with wonder and regret of Tan, who had shared his life for so many years. "I miss him."

"He must have had some dragon spirit in him," Sesshin remarked. "Somehow I failed to notice that while he was alive, though I knew he was an exceptional man. I perceive much more clearly now I am blind. This young man is your son?"

"Yes, his name is Takeyoshi."

"I can tell you have a kind heart," Sesshin said to Take. "Try not to make as many mistakes as your father."

"He is not cursed with the powers of sorcery," Shika replied. "He will be a warrior, I hope."

"Even monkeys fall from trees," Sesshin said. "Even warriors make mistakes. And your powers have blessed you as much as they have cursed you. Your biggest mistake was not getting rid of those imps, while you had the chance."

"We would never have rescued Yoshimori without their help," Shika said with assumed mildness.

"Well, it's too late now. They are in the world and you will have to live with that."

They reached the gate, which was guarded by one of Kiku's men, who had a powerfully muscled upper body and only one leg. Shika had seen him in action and knew he hopped faster than most men could run.

Sesshin sniffed the air rudely. "I smell one of their men here. You may find you want to deal with that as soon as possible."

Shika was surprised and a little disconcerted to see Kiku's man here at the temple's gate. He had not known the Crippled Army had taken over Ryusonji. He felt a moment of disquiet that Kiku might know enough of sorcery to tap into the sacred power of the temple and gain access to the same supernatural skills as the Prince Abbot.

The guard recognized him and made a clumsy bow.

"You will find Master Kikuta inside, lord."

I must order Master Kikuta *back to Kitakami*, Shika thought. *I cannot have him here.*

As they walked through the first courtyard Sesshin said, "Aritomo's men broke my lute. I wonder if there is another one lying around. I miss playing. I discovered music late in life, but it became my greatest pleasure. I used to sit just over there, facing the garden and the lake. I sang to the dragon child. I like to think it pleased him and consoled him."

"You should have Genzo," Take said. "That's the imperial lute that Lady Hina hid for years."

"Yes, I know all about Genzo, but I think a lute that is not enchanted would suit me better."

Shika looked over at the lake, now brimming with water, and saw Hina.

Leaving Take to accompany Sesshin to the temple, he walked toward her. At the sound of his footsteps, she turned her head.

Frost lay on the ground and etched the bare branches of the maples and the edge of the lake. It had grown much colder. *I should put my arms around her and warm her,* he thought. Instead he bowed formally.

"Lady Hina."

She smiled slightly. "I come to this place frequently. I feel very close to my father and my brother here."

"Will you stay in the capital?"

She looked at him steadily for a few moments and then said quietly, "I don't know where else to go. I am not sure what place there is for a woman with my past."

"You are Lord Kiyoyori's daughter. Nothing can change that. You are the heir to his estates."

"I cannot live at Matsutani. It has too many unhappy

memories. I will give the estates to the Emperor and he can bestow them where he wishes."

"He will not wish to bestow them anywhere," Shika said bitterly, "as he does not wish to be emperor."

"Unless you are brought up with the knowledge from childhood it must be unbearable," she replied. "But what else can he do? He cannot run away and live with the monkeys again. And if he did, what would it all have been for?" She gestured at the temple and the lake, "All the sacrifices, all the deaths?"

He could think of nothing to say.

Hina looked at him with concern. "What brings you here? Was it to talk to Master Kikuta? He seems to have settled in here."

"I did not know that until now."

"Does it alarm you?" she said astutely.

"A little."

"You should beware of him," she said.

"I know he has become very powerful." Shikanoko sighed. "I must talk to him, but first I have a small ceremony to perform. The guardian spirits from Matsutani are still in my weapons. I would leave them there—at least I could keep an eye on them and control them, and I am grateful for how they saved our lives on the riverbank—but my sword, Jato, is now my son's, and it is too much for him. I met Master Sesshin on the way here and he agrees they should be placed somewhere safe here. They will have to obey him."

"Sesshin?" Hina looked past him to the temple. "I have

the eyes here with me. I did not know what to do with them."

"Give them back to him," Shika said.

"Yes, that seems right." She called out, "Ibara, would you mind bringing the bamboo box to me?"

Ibara came out of the shadow of the cloister. She bowed her head to Shika as she passed him and murmured, "Lord."

He hardly recognized her. The woman's clothes she wore seemed to shrink her physically, softened her features, made her submissive, turned her into a servant.

Have we all imprisoned ourselves, become captives of the roles we have to assume?

"Sesshin is on the veranda with Take," he said to Hina, following her as she walked swiftly to the others.

She knelt and touched her brow to the ground. "Master, it is I, Hina."

"Hina? Kiyoyori's child? The little girl who tried to be a healer? Well, well, what a surprise! Though I shouldn't say that, because, really, it is no surprise at all. It all turns out the way it is meant to be."

"I have brought your eyes," Hina said, taking his hands and placing them around the bamboo box. "And I want to thank you for the Kudzu Vine Treasure Store."

"You managed to read it? I thought you would. Though why I should have thought that, I don't know, as no one else has ever managed it, apart from me." His fingers fumbled with the lid. He opened it and the eyes looked out as bright and lustrous as ever.

None of them said anything for a few moments, silenced

by what the eyes showed them, the brief and fragile nature of their lives, the futility of all their striving.

But Shika saw something more. He saw his own heart, his love and need for Hina, and he knew she saw her love for him, too.

"Well," Sesshin said. "It's taken you long enough to realize it, my boy, but it's been your destiny ever since you rode into Matsutani on that bad-tempered brown mare."

He closed the box. "I don't need these. As I said, I see more clearly without them. I will put them where they can make sure those rascals behave themselves." He reached out to Hina and Shikanoko, as though he would join their hands, but he was interrupted by a voice calling down the cloisters.

"Shikanoko! You are here at last!"

Kiku hurried eagerly toward them. "Welcome! Come inside, let me get you something to eat and drink." His eyes fell on Sesshin. "Who is this old man?"

"This is Master Sesshin," Shika said. "One of your fathers, as it happens."

A shadow passed over Kiku's face. "I remember now. We freed him, and in return he told you to kill us."

"He didn't mean it, and he's sorry now," Shika said.

"I did mean it and I'm not sorry," Sesshin said. "But I accept your existence now and I'll try to work around it."

"I'm glad to hear it," Kiku said. "All the same, I don't think I want you here. Get moving, get out."

When Sesshin did not stand up, Kiku called, "Tsune-tomo! Throw him out!"

"He is a great sorcerer," Shika said. "He goes where he wants to go, and stays where he wants to stay."

"Does he want to go to Paradise?" Tsunetomo appeared with drawn sword.

"Ha-ha!" Sesshin rocked with laughter. "I'd be very grateful if you could send me there."

"He cannot be killed," Shika explained.

"Really?" Kiku put out a hand to restrain Tsunetomo, who seemed eager to test Shika's claim. "That's interesting. You may stay then, as long as you don't get in my way."

"Kiku," Shika said, "it is not for you to decide at Ryusonji who stays and who leaves. I want you to go back to Kitakami. You have carved out a place for yourself there; no one is going to challenge you on that or take it from you. You must leave the capital with all your men before the end of the month."

Kiku stared at him. "I like it here. This is a place of great power. I can use that."

"I will not allow Ryusonji to become a center of sorcery again. That is over. From now on, it will be a place of worship, nothing more."

"Any power I gain here, from the dragon child or whatever other source, would be at your service. We would all work for you, as we have done till now. You could achieve anything you wanted with our help." Kiku's voice had a faint note of pleading to it now. There was something incongruous to it, as though he were still a child, which of course, in human terms, he was, just an adolescent, not much older than Take. The thought touched Shika deeply. He had brought them up as his sons; he still felt a responsibility for Kiku, and for Mu and Kuro, who had now come silently along the veranda to stand at their brother's side.

"I am truly grateful to you all," he said. "Our lives have been entwined for years, ever since you were born, and there are strong bonds between us. But I do not want you in the capital, least of all at Ryusonji, certainly not with Gessho's skull. My order stands: leave before the end of the month."

"We are your sons," Kiku said stubbornly. "Look, I have brought back the carving. I saw it on the werehawk's leg and knew it was a message from you. I came at once with all my men. We saved your life, we saved the Emperor."

"I told you," Mu interrupted. "He has a human son. He will never need you, or love you, in that way. Let's go back to Kitakami. The Tribe, your tribe, can flourish and be strong there."

Kiku's gaze turned to Take, who was still kneeling beside Sesshin, the sword Jato lying next to him on the boards. He let the carving fall from his fingers, stepped toward him, and dropped to one knee, staring intently into his face.

"Let me see what a human son looks like," he whispered.

Take tried to cry out, then his eyes began to roll back in his head. Faster than the snake that was forged within it, Jato rose and thrust itself into the space between them, breaking the Kikuta gaze.

Kiku grasped the sword with both hands, trying to push it away, but it resisted him. Blood began to seep from his palms.

Take came half-awake and made a grab for the hilt. "Let go!"

Kiku made no response, concentrating on dominating

the sword. Shika could feel the power he possessed, emanating from him, the power that came from the skull, the sorcery and wisdom of the Old People. Shika had not realized Kiku was so strong. His heart quailed momentarily. He was not ready for yet another challenge. "Master," he whispered, "do something."

"I gave all my power to you, remember?" Sesshin said cheerfully. "It's up to you now."

Almost without thinking, Shika opened the seven-layered bag and took out the mask. He looked across at Kiku. Their eyes met. Jato hovered motionless.

"You don't want to use it, do you?" Kiku said. "So give it to me." He twisted the sword and it struggled from Take's grasp. Kiku took it, the blood seeping from the horizontal cuts across both palms. "Give it to me or your human son dies."

"Don't give it to him," Hina cried.

Shika put the mask to his face and felt it cleave to him. He feared it might be for the last time, that Kiku's power would be greater than his, and he would never be able to remove the mask again. He saw years of loneliness and grief stretching away before him. But then he realized that it was more powerful than ever, that those years in the Darkwood had refined and honed it, as they had him. *Anything is possible to me*, he thought with wonder and awe. He said silently, *Put the sword down!* And then aloud, "Hidari-sama! Come here!"

Kiku's face twisted in pain, as he lost the struggle with the sword and relinquished it with an anguished cry, staring in shock at the bloody lines on his hands.

Jato, which had been about to plunge into Take's throat, flew from Kiku's hand to Shika's.

"You will obey me," he said, and Kiku bowed his head. His eyes glistened with tears though he did not let them fall.

"What happened?" Hidarisama exclaimed. "That was close!"

"You idiot," said Migisama. "You nearly made a big mistake. You were obeying the wrong person."

"Oof! Maybe it's time to get out of this sword."

"Before you do any harm."

"Now I will do what I came to do," Shika said. "Hidarisama, you are to stay here. Choose where you want to go."

"What about me?" said Migisama. "Don't I get to choose?"

"Shikanoko was talking to me!"

"You're the one who did something stupid, not me."

"Make up your minds quickly," Shika said. "How about the pagoda? Or the main gates?"

"The gates, so we can watch everyone go in and out."

"The pagoda, so we can see the whole city."

"If it's the pagoda, I want the top."

"Why should you have the top? You wanted the gates."

"You may go to the pagoda," Shika said. "You can share the top floor. Hidarisama will have the waxing moon, Migisama the waning."

"Oh, very well."

"I suppose that's acceptable."

The voices of the guardian spirits grew fainter.

"Hey, he didn't say what happens when there's no moon."

"We'll come down then and have fun!"

There was a slight movement of the ground like a small earthquake as the pagoda quivered. A flock of white doves that had been dozing on the roof flew up with a sudden fluttering of wings. As if they had pierced the clouds, a few large flakes of snow began to fall.

Kiku looked at his palms, now marked forever with bloody wounds that would fade into distinctive scars. "I will do as you command," he said, "but I will never forgive you. You and I are enemies from now on, as will be our children and our children's children."

"Those children will all bear the mark of the sword," Sesshin remarked. "Long after what caused it has been forgotten."

Kiku turned abruptly and walked away, disappearing into the main hall. Tsunetomo went after him. Kuro looked at Shika, seemed about to say something, then changed his mind and followed his brother.

Mu said, "We will leave today to get back to Kitakami before winter sets in."

"You may stay in the city," Shika said.

"Do you fear me less than you fear him?" Mu looked at him with an amused expression.

"It's not fear," Shika replied, but in fact it was a kind of fear, of what Kiku might become, mingled with love and regret, bringing him close to tears. "But there is a difference between you."

"Maybe because I was lucky enough to cross paths with a tengu," Mu said.

Shika nodded, remembering Shisoku's words from long

ago and, earlier, the fawn's form, the tengu overhead, the game of Go.

"I'll go with him," Mu said. "I'll try to explain everything to him. There are many things he doesn't understand."

"I'm coming with you," Ibara said.

"That would be most pleasant." Mu was smiling. "You can meet my daughter, and my youngest brother, Ku."

"I'm sick of being a woman, and—forgive me, Lady Hina, I don't mean to offend you—a servant. I liked it in the forest when I was equal to men."

"Maybe we will go back to the forest," Mu said, with a trace of longing. "We should see how things are at the old hut, and how Ima is getting on. But for a little while we must stay with Kiku."

Hina spoke quietly behind Shika. "Come to me. I will remove the mask."

He turned and bowed his head, feeling deep relief as it slid easily from his face. He took it from her, feeling the cool touch of her fingers, and slipped it into the seven-layered bag.

"I was afraid he would take it from you," she whispered, "even kill you for it."

"He nearly succeeded," he said in a low voice. He was trembling with exhaustion.

"Can someone tell me what happened?" Take said, looking as if he had just woken up.

"Kiku put you to sleep with his gaze," Mu said. "I've seen him do it before."

"I felt I knew nothing, had learned nothing, from you or the tengu," Take said, shamefaced.

"Well, learn from this experience," Mu said. "Never let anyone from the Kikuta family look you in the eyes."

"Hidarisama has left the sword," Shika said, handing Jato back to Take. "You may use it freely." *Now I will speak to Hina*, he thought. *Now we will walk down to the lake together and discuss our future.*

As though she read his mind she looked up at him and smiled. Her hand touched his briefly. He heard his heart pounding, but it was not his heart, it was hoofbeats. A horse neighed and Nyorin answered, from where he was waiting outside the gate.

"Nagatomo is here!" Take cried.

The Burnt Twins came through the main gate on horseback, allowing no one to stop them. The horses were breathing hard, eyes wild, flanks heaving. Nagatomo dismounted, approached Shika, and said quietly, "The Emperor has disappeared."

Eisei slid from his horse's back. "Saru has vanished, too."

"How could that happen?" Shika said with quiet anger. "Must I look after everything myself?"

"No one expected them to be so agile, so acrobatic," Nagatomo replied. "They scaled the wall, leaped into a tree, and were away over the river before anyone could follow. Apparently a young woman was waiting on the far bank with a change of clothes. We found the Emperor's robes abandoned there."

"We must go after him," Shika said.

"I've told people he is unwell," Nagatomo said. "We should not let the news spread, and we cannot pursue him as if he were a criminal."

"I'll go and find him," Take said. "I can persuade him to return."

Shikanoko looked at his son for a moment without speaking. "Very well," he said finally. "There's no point in me going, as he hates me above all. But you knew him in his other life. If he listens to anyone, it will be you. But who will go with you?"

"Lend me Nyorin. I will go alone. Don't worry, Father. I know both the riverbank and the forest. I know where they will go."

20

TAKEYOSHI

As Takeyoshi followed the river north the snow continued to fall, but it was not settling enough to reveal tracks. He had Jato at his hip and Ameyumi on his back. He rode at a canter, trusting the old horse not to stumble, and, if anyone greeted him, he replied it was a good day for hunting. He wore the bearskin chaps that the tengu had given him and a green robe that had belonged to Hina's father, Lord Kiyoyori. After a while the snow stopped, the clouds cleared a little, and a pale wintry sun appeared. There was no wind.

The Sagigawa flowed from Lake Kasumi to the capital. Between the river and the mountains of the Darkwood lay a pattern of rice fields and vegetable gardens, crisscrossed by dikes and footpaths. Take wondered if Yoshi and Saru had run through them to reach the forest, but he then thought they were more likely to be trying to get to the lake, perhaps heading for the Rainbow Bridge or Aomizu, places they knew well and where they would be hidden. As he rode he reflected on the grief they must both be feeling. No one had considered the deaths of Asagao and several of the other acrobats and musicians as very important, but to the two young men they were friends, family, colleagues. He and Hina had rescued the survivors, tended their broken bodies, and arranged for the dead to be buried. They had attended their funerals and said prayers for them, but they had followed the usual temple ceremony. Take, alone, was familiar with the prayers of the Secret One, but he repeated them only in his heart.

Kai had come to Yoshi to help him get away. She had made the journey pregnant and alone. He was amazed and impressed by her devotion, and concerned for her and the unborn child.

They are going to Aomizu, he realized. *They will seek out the old priest, the one who told me not to be angry. They will tell the families how the others died, ask for forgiveness, and pray with them. They will hide, like all the other runaways and outcasts, among the people of the riverbank.*

Just before the barrier at Kasumiguchi he saw Kon flying overhead. The sight of the bird comforted him. It meant he was going in the right direction. Kon would lead him to Yoshimori.

The barrier was still guarded by Kiku's men. They were stopping people and demanding, "Red or White? The new emperor or the old?" as though all alternatives had been reduced to a single choice: True or false? Right or wrong? How did anyone know ultimately?

They were persuaded by Take's excuse of hunting, and let him through as they did most of the common people. They were concerned only with arresting fleeing Miboshi warriors.

Yoshi and Saru would have looked like the many ragged youths who were walking in either direction, to the capital to sell produce and firewood, or going home to their villages.

After the barrier he let Nyorin walk for a while to rest him. Gradually the road became less crowded. There were fewer villages, the land was wilder and more mountainous. He had grown more used to being alone, but as night fell the solitude of the landscape began to make him uneasy. He tried to sing to raise his spirits, but all the songs he knew reminded him of the dead musicians. He seemed to hear their voices echoing from the darkness, the ghostly strain of a lute, the rhythmic beating of a drum. He felt Kai was ahead of him, and the drum was hers.

The moon rose, casting shadows of horse and rider on the frosty ground. He did not want to stop, it was too cold, so he let the horse walk on. From time to time he dozed a little, feeling his head grow heavy and his eyelids close. He smelled smoke, not sure if he was waking or dreaming, and heard a rattle and clicking of stones.

Nyorin came to a halt, pricked up his ears, and turned his head. Take looked in the same direction and saw a shadowy figure silhouetted against the firelight. He recognized the bulky outline, the beaked head.

"Tadashii!" he said. Nyorin gave a low whinny and stepped purposefully toward the fire.

"Ah, here you are," the tengu said. "Come and sit down. Meet my friend—actually, I think you met, after a fashion, before. He doesn't have a human name, but that doesn't matter. He doesn't speak and, anyway, you will never see him again after tonight. We are just passing the time until . . . well, never mind what, just passing the time in a game of Go."

The board was carved on the stump of a kawa tree, the white stones were shells, gleaming with mother-of-pearl, the black ones were obsidian pebbles, river smooth. They rested in bowls of mulberry wood, reflecting in the firelight.

Tadashii rattled the black stones in his bowl. His opponent grunted in irritation and rolled his eyes.

"It's considered very rude to do that," Tadashii said. "But I like to annoy him."

He picked up a black stone and placed it on the board with a loud clack.

"This is you," he whispered. "I knew you were on your way, but he didn't. You getting the Rain Bow upset him, but this will shock him, even more! Oooh, now we are in the endgame!"

He laughed loudly, the sound echoing back from the cliff face as though twenty tengu were laughing with him.

"Wait," Take said. "Why am I a piece in your game?"

"Don't worry about it," the tengu replied. "Rest by the fire. I think there's a flask of cold broth and some bones left if you're hungry. Tomorrow it will all work out, you'll see."

Take's eyelids were drooping against his will. He barely found the strength to unsaddle Nyorin. The old horse shook himself, exhaled heavily, and lay down. Take drank the broth and ate the rice balls he had brought with him. He cracked open the bones with his teeth and sucked the marrow from them. He had no idea what animal they were from. Then he lay down next to Nyorin, resting his head on the horse's shoulder. He heard the rattle and clack of the stones through his dreams.

Toward dawn he heard Kon calling and felt the beat of wings on his face. When he woke the tengu were gone. The embers of the fire were still warm and the tree stump remained, but it was no longer carved into a grid nor was there any sign of the shells and stones.

Was the game over? Had they moved on to play somewhere else? Or had he just dreamed it all?

Nyorin got stiffly to his feet, snorted, and let out a stream of urine, which steamed in the freezing air.

"I suppose we must go on," Take said, lifting the saddle to place it on the stallion's back.

Something, or someone, had left a trail on the ground. At first he thought they were shells, gleaming white, but when he saw them more clearly he realized they were feathers, each tip spotted with purple.

Did tengu bleed? Had Tadashii pulled feathers from his wings to show Take the way? He was touched by this sacrifice, but then it occurred to him the tengu would do anything to win the game.

The trail led to a clearing by a small pool. It was full of birds, blue and white herons. They all had their heads turned in one direction, watching two young men on the bank. Kai sat on the edge of the pool, her head turned, like the birds', toward Yoshi and Saru. Her hair covered her like a cloak. Her feet were bare. *How beautiful she is*, he thought with a surge of longing.

Yoshi and Saru were walking on their hands, reflecting each other's movements with perfect symmetry. It was a routine he remembered, but it seemed empty and sad, lacking the older men and the monkeys. He could move in and take part as he used to, but he had vowed he would never do acrobatics again. That part of his life was over. It was over for Yoshi and Saru, too. No matter how hard they tried to re-create it, as they were doing now, it was gone.

A shadow darkened overhead. The birds all took off at once, crying in alarm. A huge tengu, Tadashii's opponent, swooped down and seized Yoshi by the feet with its talons.

Saru flipped over, screaming, and leaped to grab Yoshi's hands. The unexpected weight made the tengu falter, but its wings began to beat more powerfully. Kai leaped to her feet, calling for help.

Take pulled the bow, Ameyumi, from his back and fitted the arrow to the cord, with steady hands.

Kon flew screeching at the tengu's head.

Take aimed at the body, hoping not to hit the bird. The arrow thrummed loudly above Kon's cries and Kai's screams. The tengu made a hideous noise and opened its claws, letting Yoshi and Saru fall heavily to the ground. Then it pulled out the arrow and threw it away, drew its sword, and flew toward Take.

Nyorin reared, striking out with his front hoofs. In that moment Take slipped from his back, dropped the bow, and drew Jato. The sword came alive in his hand, just as the tengu delivered a savage blow at his head. He parried it, felt the shock run up to his shoulder, then jumped sideways as the backward sweep of the tengu's sword nearly took off his arm.

For a few moments he fought instinctively and defensively, then gradually, as time stretched out, he recalled the teachings of both Mu and Tadashii. He recovered his stance and began to notice the tengu's weaknesses. The arrow had done some damage and the tengu was losing blood—*so they definitely do bleed, purple*—and despite its enormous strength, it was slower than he was.

Kon, meanwhile, was doing his best to distract the tengu, making fluttering attacks at its face and neck. The herons returned, with their long beaks and harsh cries, and, at Kai's urging, flew at the tengu, further disabling it. It slashed out at them angrily and one fell flapping to the ground, but in that moment Jato found the unprotected chest and thrust upward through the ribs to the heart.

Blood gushed out, purple and frothy, but still the tengu did not die. It threw its sword at Take and, with a look of hatred in its eyes, made a gesture of surrender and farewell. Its wings moved slowly, barely enough to lift it from the ground and clear the treetops, its feet scraping through the branches, blood dripping in large spots like summer rain.

A noise came from the mountains, an echo of Tadashii's laughter. *Maybe I just won your game for you*, Take thought, *but now I have my own endgame to play.*

Yoshi and Saru lay on the ground, unmoving. For a

moment he was afraid the fall had killed them, but then Saru moaned and he saw Yoshi's eyes flicker open. He knew he should kneel and offer his sword to the Emperor, but his fury got the better of him.

"You nearly got me killed! The birds of the air came to my aid! You could not defend yourself or help me?"

He looked at the dying heron with sorrow. "Even the heron knows who you are and gave its life for you. Kon has followed you loyally for years. Won't you recognize that, admit you are the Emperor and accept it?"

For a few moments Yoshi did not reply. A deep silence filled the clearing. No birds called; even Kon was mute.

Then the Emperor got to his feet and walked toward Kai. He held her in a close embrace, swept back her hair, and kissed her ears. He whispered something to her and she looked at Take and nodded, tears pouring from her eyes. The Emperor glanced at the heron and at Kon and then turned to Takeyoshi.

"Kai does not want to be an emperor's concubine. I am entrusting her to you. Bring the child up as your own. Maybe one day, if she agrees, you will marry. To honor the heron you will take it as your crest, and, as your name, Otori, like the houou that Kon has become. Now help me onto the horse."

Otori Takeyoshi bowed and obeyed, then lifted Kai up behind Yoshimori.

"You can walk." The Emperor turned the stallion's head and rode in the direction of the capital, Take on one side, Saru on the other, the golden houou flying overhead.

21

SHIKANOKO

The Emperor acted as he had threatened, and his first act, after ascending the Lotus Throne, was to exile Shikanoko from the city. Next he granted lands in the extreme west to Iida no Saru and Otori Takeyoshi, in the wild area that would come to be known as the Three Countries. In exchange for her estates of Matsutani and Kuromori, and in recognition of her family's sacrifices and losses, he gave the domain of Maruyama, where her mother had been born, to Kiyoyori's daughter, Lady Hina, stipulating only that it should always be inherited through the female line.

It was as though he wanted no one around him who knew what he had been formerly, nothing to remind him of all he had lost.

The Kakizuki lords ran the city as they had before, taking over Aritomo's improved administration and more productive taxation system, and continuing to love music, poetry, and dancing as much as ever.

Eisei became the abbot at Ryusonji and, with the advice of Sesshin, developed a close enough relationship with the dragon child to ensure its blessings and protection. The two werehawks lived with them. He and Sesshin also composed *The Tale of Shikanoko*: the ballads of the Emperor of the Eight Islands, the Autumn Princess and the Dragon Child, the Lord of the Darkwood, and the Tengu's Game of Go, as they are known today.

Nagatomo went to Maruyama with Lady Hina.

In Kitakami, Mu and Kiku disagreed about everything until Mu—Master Muto by now—moved with Ibara and their children to Hagi, where Otori Takeyoshi was building a castle. Take's courageous and cheerful nature had endeared him to the natives of his new land. He knew that life was like a game of Go, complex and demanding, but still only a game, and he was determined to play it as best he could. He and Kai came to love each other, marry, and have many children.

Kinpoge married her cousin Juntaro, but her life and Take's continued to be entwined, one with the other. The tengu Tadashii had been wrong, for once, when he said they would not see each other again.

Shikanoko spent more than a year on a lonely island off the far southern coast, with only Gen for company apart from the islanders, who taught him ways to fish, as well as various secrets and spells that calmed storms and summoned sea monsters. It amused him that he had, indeed, straddled the Eight Islands, from north to south, as Kongyo had dreamed, but as an exile not as a ruler. Somewhat against his wishes, he gained a reputation for wisdom and power, and in his second spring on the island he began to receive many visitors seeking help and advice.

One of these came in the third month, when the island's surface was covered with tiny purple and yellow flowers and the air was filled with the chirping of seabird chicks. He wore a black silk covering over his face.

Gen wagged his wispy tail and whimpered.

"Nagatomo!" Shikanoko said in delight, and embraced his old friend. "What brings you here?"

"It seems you have been pardoned, to the extent that you may leave the island, though you may not return to the capital."

"I hope I never visit that place again in my life!" Shikanoko replied. "But where am I to go?"

"Anywhere you like, west of the High Cloud Mountains."

Shikanoko was silent, remembering, reflecting. Then he said, "So I am never to see the Darkwood again, nor Kumayama?"

Nagatomo did not reply directly but said, "Lady Hina sent me."

"Is she well?"

"She invites you to Maruyama. She said to tell you she must have a daughter to inherit the domain, but a daughter cannot be born without a father."

Shikanoko smiled and said, "She must have hundreds clamoring to be her husband."

"She will marry no one but you," Nagatomo said. "My opinion is, you owe it to future generations."

"So I do," Shika agreed. He was imagining his daughters, as wise and beautiful as Hina, as brave as Takeyoshi. And then he remembered Hina's hands on his face as she removed the mask, and a wave of hope and longing swept over him.

"We will leave on the next tide," he said.

AUTHOR'S NOTE

The Tale of Shikanoko was partly inspired by the great medieval warrior tales of Japan: *The Tale of the Heike, The Taiheiki,* the tales of Hōgen and Heiji, the *Jōkyūki,* and *The Tale of the Soga Brothers.* I have borrowed descriptions of weapons and clothes from these and am indebted to their English translators Royall Tyler, Helen Craig McCullough, and Thomas J. Cogan.

I would like to thank in particular Randy Schadel, who read early versions of the novels and made many invaluable suggestions.

All four volumes of Lian Hearn's
The Tale of Shikanoko will be published in 2016.

EMPEROR OF THE EIGHT ISLANDS
April 2016

AUTUMN PRINCESS, DRAGON CHILD
June 2016

LORD OF THE DARKWOOD
August 2016

THE TENGU'S GAME OF GO
September 2016

FSG Originals
www.fsgoriginals.com